DESCENDANTS OF WRATH

TONY CONTRATTO

The Fourth Book of
The Agents of Fate Series

Hensley de Vere Press
Lake Havasu City, AZ

DESCENDANTS OF WRATH
Copyright © 2024 Tony Contratto

ISBN 979-8-9886090-7-0 (Paperback)

Library of Congress Control Number: 2024922921

First paperback and e-book editions November 2024

Cover art by: Nora Hutton, Muenz/Getty Images
(used under license)

Edited by: Kim Beckham

Printed in the United States of America

Hensley de Vere Press LLC
1799 Kiowa Ave
Suite 111
Lake Havasu City, AZ 86403
hensleydevere.com
contact@hensleydevere.com

Dedication

Adalyn

Mais tout de suite, tu as été ma petite princesse, mon cœur

CONTENTS

Preface

When I originally thought up the idea and story for Agents of Fate back in college, I envisioned Hayden de Vere as the "main character." True to [most of] my original ideas, that is how the first book turned out. I actually wrote *Agents of Fate* and *The Princess of Time* at the same time. Most of the characters were in my imagination already. Although some of them didn't have names yet, characters like Hayden, Paige, Dan, and Kali had been there for years. Abby was a newcomer as I wrote the story. The idea of Armond was there, but he needed a name and more backstory. One of the characters that I had never dreamt up, until I started writing, was Elle. She quickly became one of my favorite characters. I must admit that I admire Elle... her fortitude, grace, and empathy.

With the arrival of Book Four, we will meet Hayden and Elle's second-born daughter. Her personality is a sort of eclectic mix of brash and endearing. She is smart, strong, and willing to fight for what she believes is right. I originally thought that Hayden was the main character. His daughter is challenging that assumption in my own mind.

I hope you enjoy the fourth entry in the Series, which we will soon conclude with Book Five: Child of Hope.

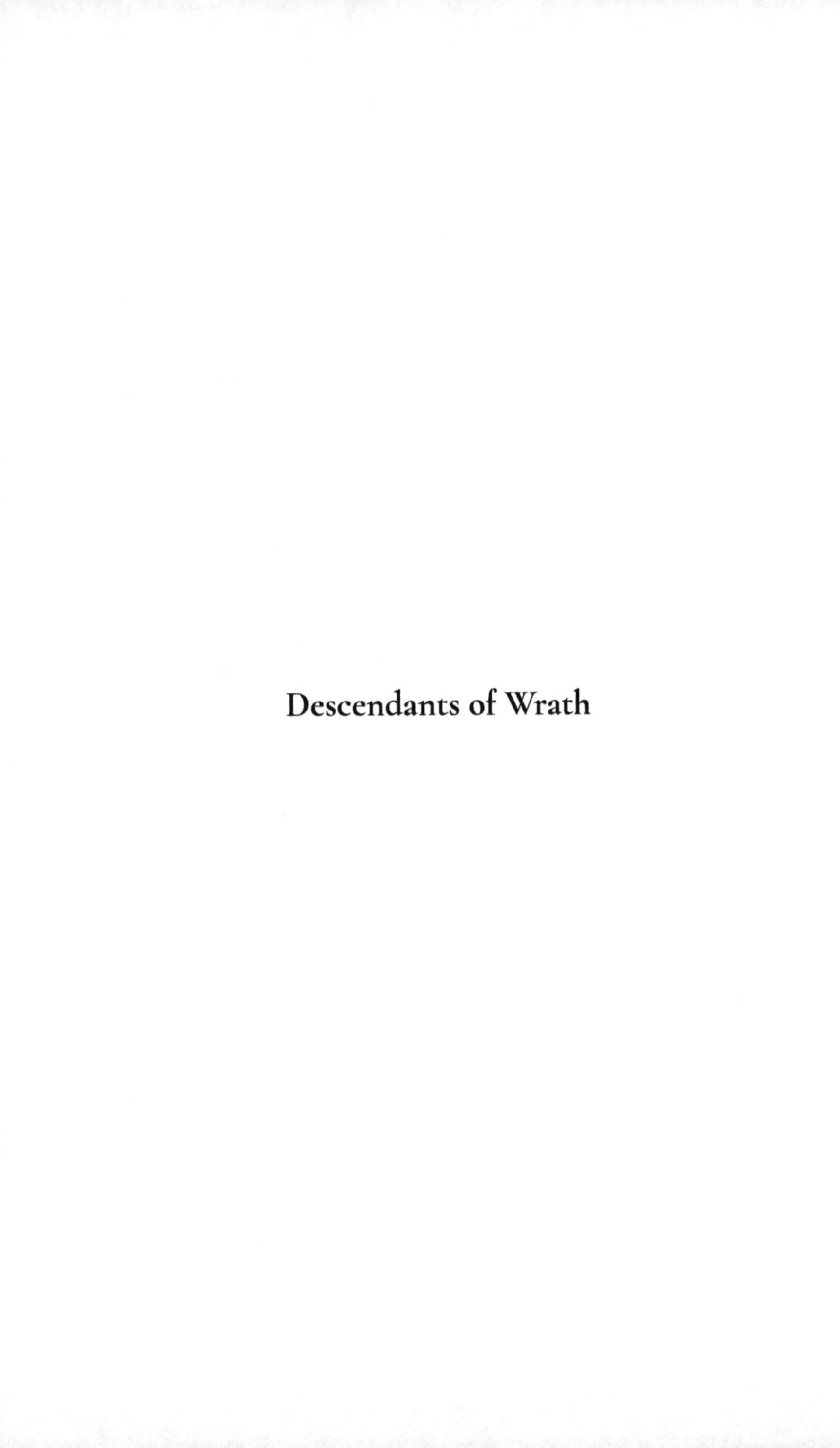

Descendants of Wrath

اسبيل

Chapter One

A'ltal Bilv'at

A bright flash of purple light erupted in the center of a crumbling building. Hayden stepped out of a portal and immediately confronted Amaris, who had Kiera at his side.

"Give me my daughter back!" Hayden yelled at Amaris.

"I don't believe that she wants to go with you," Amaris said with a wry smile painted on his face.

"Come on, Kiera, we are going back home," Hayden insisted as he walked up to her.

"I'm not going anywhere with you," she protested. "I am here with Amaris. I love him."

"That is nonsense," Hayden replied as he reached out his hand for hers. "Let's go."

Kiera pulled away and reached under Amaris' coat, producing a dagger that she held firmly to her own throat. Hayden stood and analyzed the situation, determining that she must be under Amaris' control.

"Like I said before, I don't think she wants to go with you," Amaris said as he chuckled.

"What did you do to her?" Hayden demanded to know.

"Well, it's simple enough," Amaris said. "If Kiera is outside a certain range from me, she will take her own life… by whatever means necessary. So I wouldn't come back and try to steal her away in the night either."

"Kiera, baby girl," Hayden said empathetically. "I will figure out a way to get you out of here."

"Good luck with that," Amaris said.

"If you touch her, I will…"

"I know, I know," Amaris interrupted. "Torture me slowly, make me wish I was dead, so on and so forth. Kiera isn't playing that role in my plan. She's an insurance policy. Stay out of my way and she stays alive."

Hayden begrudgingly opened a portal back to 2024 and stepped inside to explain the situation to Elle.

જી જી જી જી જી જી

56,005 BC

A light breeze caressed the flourishing valley. The grasses on either side of a meager, yet well-traveled, dirt path waved along with the wind's flowing symphony. It was a mild day. A gentle current of air washed over a caravan of traders that slowly trudged on over the peak of a nearby hill before descending into the valley. In contrast with the lush collection of grass on the valley floor, only a singular tree stood in the space between the peaks of two strikingly similar hilltops.

The road was one that this caravan had traveled many times before as they brought goods and spices from other regions back to their homeland. As with most of their journeys, the group passed the time by singing songs and recounting stories. They had all heard the stories before, but that fact didn't keep them from sharing them again. The chatter amongst the group ceased when one of the men pointed to the sky. Above the horizon, a pulsing light had become visible.

"It is just a bright star, still lingering on in the daylight," one of the men said dismissively.

"No, it is not," the man who had pointed out the strange phenomenon argued. "Look there, it is moving. It is getting closer to us."

The traders focused in their vision and fixated on the alleged movement of the strange object. Thirty seconds later, everyone was convinced that it was indeed moving toward them.

"What is it?" the doubter asked.

No one bothered to attempt an answer. The traders watched in awe as the object became clearer. It was a fireball streaking through the otherwise peaceful sky. Their awe turned to tentative fear when they realized that the object was still moving toward them.

"Get to cover!" the leader of the caravan said to the others.

"There is no cover in this valley!" one of the other men reminded him.

Their hurried shuffling about the valley floor was in vain. The object was quickly advancing on their coordinates. Several of the men stood and watched, realizing that any attempt to flee was just a futile use of energy. To their bewilderment, the flaming object appeared to slow as it approached overhead. The fire surrounding the object extinguished, leaving a translucent bubble that now slowly descended to the ground. It came to rest underneath the branches of the lone tree gracing the valley floor. The group sprinted toward the tree to investigate.

"There is something in there," one of the men said as they neared the object.

The bubble-like field flickered away and revealed a young woman, crouched in the tall grasses surrounding the tree. She remained motionless for several minutes before finally rising to her feet.

"A'ltal alsamawat tahtah Bilva," the caravan leader said as the woman approached them.

"Bilva?" the woman uttered her first word.

"Yes, Bilva," the man confirmed as he pointed to the tree to indicate its species. "You are the powers of the heavens descended underneath the Bilva tree. Who are you?"

"You may call me Bilv'at," the woman replied. "Are you the leader of your people?"

"Me?" the caravan leader replied. "I am only the leader of this caravan. I am not the leader of our people. He resides in our main city. We are headed back to the city now."

"Will you take me there with you?" Bilv'at asked.

"We will, if you wish," the man agreed. "We still have a long journey ahead of us. It is almost a forty-day walk, one thousand miles, from this valley to 'Ain Ghazal."

"I will be fine," Bilv'at said. "I will accompany you."

❧ ❧ ❧ ❧ ❧ ❧

Forty days later - The City of 'Ain Ghazal

The weary caravan of traders plodded along, each footstep along the familiar hill heavier than the last. From the west, the light breeze carried promises of their homeland. As they crested the peak, their destination came into view. Bilv'at scanned the scene in front of her and saw the wide-open fields, dotted with livestock. At the terminus of their route stood a walled city. From their vantage point some five hundred yards away, the sounds and scents of the town filled their senses.

As the group approached the city walls, a large gathering of children, wives, and friends hurried out to greet them. Bilv'at watched as families reunited. Some of the children seemed to be particularly interested in her presence, a newcomer among a sea of familiar faces. The caravan leader walked over to Bilv'at, his children ducked behind him, but curiously peeked around his body to catch glimpses of the strange new woman.

"Let's get you inside to Emir Hamedi," the caravan leader told Bilv'at. "Welcome to our home, 'Ain Ghazal."

Bilv'at followed on a journey through a maze of streets, toward a large stone hall that rose above the surrounding buildings. They approached the set of tall wooden doors that provided the only relief in the stone façade. The room grew quiet as the duo entered. A man seated at the end of the hall rose from his ornately decorated chair and stared at Bilv'at and her companion.

"Saleem Amman!" the man shouted across the hall as he walked toward the duo.

"Emir," the caravan leader replied with a bowed head as the man approached.

"Saleem, welcome home," the Emir said before embracing Saleem. "I cannot wait to see what your caravan has brought back for the people of our city."

"You will be delighted to know that this journey was very fruitful," Saleem replied. "We acquired many new spices, metals, and textiles."

"We shall hold a feast for you and your comrades tomorrow evening," the Emir stated. "Now, who is this woman accompanying you?"

"This is no ordinary woman," Saleem replied. "This is Bilv'at. She descended from the heavens in a ball of fire. Her counsel and premonitions have kept us from danger several times along the journey back home. I believe that you should speak with her."

"A ball of fire?" the Emir remarked as he stepped over

and examined Bilv'at. He was not sure what to make of the tale. "Yet you remain unburnt. Tell me, who are you? Why are you here?"

"I am a messenger, a guide," Bilv'at said. As she stepped forward, her countenance changed. An aura of light seemed to radiate from her head and torso. "As Saleem said, I am here to guide you and your people. To help turn your city into a kingdom that reaches the edges of the five seas."

"That is quite the claim," Emir Hamedi told her. "Let us see how well you deliver. There is a tribe attacking one of our towns in the south. We have not been able to repel or defeat them. My advisors have different opinions on our course of action. Look at this map and tell me what I should do."

"Neither of these options will help you win," Bilv'at said as she examined the map and proposed plans. "They will expect you to use this bridge or to march down from the north. Send your forces through this range to the east of the city and descend on their army just before daylight. Send a small party of fighters to the west side of the river. They can remain undetected and intercept anyone trying to flee over the bridge."

"That would take longer, but they won't expect it," the Emir replied. "Let's try it. I will have our army march tomorrow morning. For now, have Saleem show you to a vacant home and get you a meal."

Several days later, news from the southern town of Valmare arrived. The enemy had been completely destroyed. The Emir called Bilv'at into his chambers and thanked her for her advice.

"If you desire, Emir, I can consult you on expanding your territory," Bilv'at said. "I believe that together we can build a great empire."

"What would you do to accomplish that?" the Emir asked.

Bilv'at rolled out a map of the region on the large wooden table in the center of the room. Over the next hour, she outlined a detailed plan for the Emir's army.

"This is ambitious," Emir Hamedi said cautiously. "At my age, I fear that I may not live to see it to fruition. However, the plan is well thought out. The strategy makes sense. If this works, I will have to reward you handsomely."

56,002 BC

Bilv'at stood in the center of a large tent, surrounded by the empire's chief military officials. A large map was sprawled out across the table with markers littered across its surface to designate troops, supplies, and targets.

"Over the last three years, we have managed to expand the empire a thousand miles eastward, from the sea to the gulf," Bilv'at said. "We have grown from a small collection of cities to a vast territory. Today, we begin our push southward to claim the remainder of the peninsula. We will begin with the city of Elath and then proceed southeast from there."

"We believe that all of this is attainable in the next two years?" one of the men, Fariq Masifar, asked.

"Yes," Bilv'at answered. "We were able to conquer significant amounts of territory in the last three years. Many of the towns and cities that are in the path of our new expansion plan are already willing to join the empire and are waiting for our arrival. There are several hostile targets, but the size and strength of our army far exceeds any of their forces."

"What do we anticipate in Elath?" Masifar asked.

"Elath is a small town comprising several different tribes," Bilv'at replied. "Five of the tribes are amicable to our arrival. The other three tribes are not so friendly. In the last month, our scouts and spies arrived in Elath and began spreading pro-empire propaganda. The latest reports suggest that there will be minimal fighting. We may need to make an example of some holdouts, but we will not face any considerable force."

"Are we wary of interference from the el-Abbasil Empire?" another Fariq asked.

"They have been quiet on the matter," Bilv'at said. "Our scouts report no increase in military presence along their border. I do not foresee any interference or hostilities from them. They have their own empire to attend to and have never sought to expand east of their traditional borders."

"Excellent," the Fariq said. "As requested, a detachment of two hundred soldiers are prepared for departure to Elath at sunrise. The remainder of the army will move to a rendezvous point ten miles east of the city."

"I think we are done here for the night," Bilv'at concluded. "Thank you all for your strength and loyalty. Tomorrow we will take Elath and in the coming months we will take the rest of the peninsula. I will make sure that the Emir rewards all of you handsomely for your service to the empire."

೮ ೮ ೮ ೮ ೮ ೮

The Next Morning

Bilv'at and her small force arrived at the gates of Elath. A small gathering of men stood outside the town and waited for her arrival.

"Most esteemed Bilv'at, we welcome your arrival," one of the men said as her entourage reached the gates. "I am Amadias, the leader of the Surethi tribe. It is an honor to finally meet you in person."

"What is the situation inside the city?" Bilv'at asked.

"Peaceful," Amadias replied. "There were a few holdouts among some of the tribe leaders, but we have softened their resolve in the past week and they are amenable to joining the empire. You should still meet with them as a show of good faith."

"Of course," Bilv'at responded. "Please, confer with Fariq Masifar to set up the meetings. I would like to meet with the leaders before the end of today, let's not keep anyone waiting."

"As you wish," Amadias said. "My son Istamal will show your men to the city's central district and familiarize them with the city's defense."

"Very good," Bilv'at replied. "Let us proceed."

As the group entered the city, they found the

---

streets lined with citizens. Many cheered and welcomed them in, while others stood in careful observation. The city itself was not much to speak of. The walls were perhaps the single most grand feature, constructed over several years to help put an end to a string of attacks from outside tribes. There were few other constructed buildings and it looked as though three-quarters of the population still slept in tents or makeshift dwellings. After the majority of the entourage split off, Amadias led Bilv'at and Masifar to a large building in the center of the town.

"This is the leadership chamber," Amadias said of the structure. "Tomorrow morning we have scheduled a meeting of the tribal leaders to officially cede control of the city to you and formally join the empire."

"Excellent, thank you for being so attentive," Bilv'at said. "I appreciate your help in preparing the people of Elath for our arrival. Together we will raise this city as a shining beacon of strength and prosperity for all the world to see."

"Yes, that would be most welcome," Amadias replied. "As you saw outside, the people banded together to build our fortifications. Beyond that, they never bothered to develop the rest of the city. I suppose most were content with living in tents at the time, but there is now a rapidly growing desire to build proper housing."

"Rest assured, the empire will be quick to transform this city," Bilv'at said. "We will focus on a speedy construction of dwellings for the city's citizens. Once that is completed, we will work on upgrades. The people of 'Ain Ghazal are already preparing large shipments of building materials to be accompanied by our most skilled craftsmen, merchants, builders, and healers. They will teach and mentor as they lead development."

ᴄᴈ ᴄᴈ ᴄᴈ ᴄᴈ ᴄᴈ ᴄᴈ

"Good morning," Bilv'at said to the crowd of assembled tribal leaders. "I thank you for welcoming me into your city. Though I have not yet formally met some of you here, I look forward to doing so and to working with you in the coming days and years. My name is Bilv'at and I am the emissary of 'Ain Ghazal and Emir Hamedi. We come not as conquerors or adversaries, but as partners. We welcome Elath into the new empire. Together, we will prosper and be the envy of the world."

The tribal leaders took a moment to assess their feelings toward her comments. Amadias was the first to stand and cheer in support. The remaining men in the room quickly followed his lead and the room erupted in a celebratory and raucous boom of chanting and applause. Fariq Masifar, who was sitting in a chair behind Bilv'at, observed the crowd and took notes. Next to him sat another man who had just come into the city that morning on horseback.

"The empire is in a state of constant expansion," Bilv'at continued. "Our forces that are stationed outside the city will be heading east to secure the rest of the peninsula. From 'Ain Ghazal, several more legions are heading north to expand our borders on those fronts."

"Amadias tells us that you have big plans for our city," a man sitting in the back of the room said. "What can we expect?"

"Indeed," Bilv'at replied. "I'm sorry, I do not believe we have met yet. What is your name?"

"I am Kedrinal Retamini," the man said. "My family has been in Elath for several generations. Our tribe is a thousand men strong and almost four thousand with women and children."

"Kedrinal, I thank you for your question and your hospitality," Bilv'at replied. "Our plans for Elath are grand. In the coming weeks, some of the most skilled citizens of 'Ain Ghazal will arrive. There will be builders, doctors, and teachers. We will begin construction on a new palace, expand the city walls, build schools, upgrade housing, and much more."

"What are we required to give to the empire in return?" Kedrinal asked. "There must be some sort of price for all this."

"Your skepticism is to be expected," Bilv'at replied. "It sounds too good to be true, I get that. All that is asked of the citizens of Elath is loyalty to the empire."

"Loyalty in which ways?" Kedrinal prodded.

"Other than your allegiance to the Emir and his appointees, there are a few things that we ask of you," Bilv'at continued. "The first request is that each tribe contribute a percentage of their battle trained men to the armed forces. Some will be appointed to city defense and others to the army. Behind me on the left is Fariq Masifar. He will meet with each of you to discuss this matter."

"That is a reasonable request," Kedrinal agreed.

"Excellent," Bilv'at said. "For the second request, let me introduce the person sitting next to Masifar. This is Fariq 'awal Antonus Constralis. He is one of my most trusted advisors. As is customary in many cases of new alliances, we also seek allegiance by marriage. Each tribal leader of Elath is asked to marry at least one daughter or niece to Antonus. The children of the Fariq 'awal and your kin will be appointed to rule over new cities in the empire or hold prominent posts in the army when they come of age."

"That is also fair," Kedrinal responded.

"Excellent," Bilv'at said. "Antonus will visit each of your homes in the coming days to meet your families and make arrangements. As I understand, he has already met with the Surethi family early this morning."

"Yes, he has," Amadias chimed in. "I am happy to announce that all four of my daughters will be wed to Fariq 'awal Constralis. We are truly honored to join our family's legacy with this great empire."

"In ten days we will have a ceremonial feast to celebrate with each of your families," Bilv'at continued. "Each tribe will be compensated with gold for each spouse given to Antonus. If there are no more questions, I would like to spend a few minutes getting to know each of you personally."

ɔ ɔ ɔ ɔ ɔ ɔ

Five years later

Bilv'at settled into her newly constructed dwelling in the empire's new southern capital city. Under her direction, the Emir's armies secured vast amounts of land. As his last official act before his death, the childless Emir named Bilv'at as his successor. As an act of gratitude, she named the Emir's nephew the governor of 'Ain Ghazal, which would then serve as the northern capital city of the empire.

Over the next year, visitors from throughout the region journeyed to the southern capital to greet Bilv'at. The leaders of the neighboring el-Abbasil Empire brought a large assortment of gifts and offered their friendship. Bilv'at was intrigued by their success and generosity. She learned that their empire's quick expansion was largely due to their unique abilities. Their original tribe was one of the sets of humans that had inherited the Powers of Gallitsur. Their ability to control elements like Fire, Water, and Lightning provided almost certain victory militarily.

"I have a proposition for you," Bilv'at told their leader Hal-Abbas. "I am seeking five specific artifacts that hold great significance to me. If you find these objects and bring them to me, I will reward you with a gift beyond measure."

"I do appreciate the offer," Hal-Abbas told her. "However, we already have more gold and jewels than we can count."

"I can give you something much more precious," Bilv'at said. "The ability to live for thousands of years."

"You cannot possibly grant that gift," Hal-Abbas said. "I grant that you are a great leader... a visionary even. But what you claim is not possible."

"You, who possess abilities that few other humans have ever wielded, are going to tell me that it is not possible?" Bilv'at countered. "There is magic more powerful than your own. Things that have existed long before this world. Acquire the artifacts that I desire and you will see that power. If I am lying to you and you are on your deathbed in thirty or forty years, I vow that all the land in my kingdom will be ceded to your sons."

"Your kingdom? Now that is a serious offer," Hal-Abbas replied. "Perhaps I was wrong to doubt your claims. We will seek out these artifacts and bring them to you."

೮೨ ೮೨ ೮೨ ೮೨ ೮೨ ೮೨

November 2007
Grand Marais, Minnesota

Amaris trudged through the snow covered hills as he descended toward the iced-over lake bed in front of him. In the distance, he could see two young girls frolicking about in the snow. An occasional small flash of light flickered as the girls took photographs of each other. He stepped out on the frozen lake and sped up his pace toward the girls.

"Take a picture of me on the ice!" the younger girl yelled to her sister as she skipped along the surface of the lake. Amaris was close enough now that he could just make out the words.

The young girl's stride skidded to a halt when a sharp cracking sound interrupted the gleeful moment. The ice beneath her feet gave way and she plunged into the icy water. She struggled for a few moments before slipping under. Her older sister screamed for help before running off in a panicked sprint away from the lake.

Amaris walked closer to the hole in the ice that had swallowed the young girl like death coming for a feast. The older sister returned with her parents and Amaris watched as the father dove into the freezing water.

"Call the police! Call an ambulance! Please!" a woman that Amaris recognized as the girls' mother cried out from near the hole in the ice.

Amaris ignored her calls for help. A few moments later, the sunlight that had been flooding through the picturesque landscape vanished, as if someone had flipped a lightswitch. Amaris looked over at the older sister, who was staring at him. He pointed his finger toward the sky and she looked up to see the stars blazing with intensity. Amaris glanced up and watched as one light in the sky overpowered all the others…

the brilliance of a supernova. One that would later become a supermassive black hole near the planet Moira.

The girl's gaze returned to the ice as a purple light rose from beneath it and swirled into the sky. As the wisps of light rose, the colors of the Aurora Borealis flared to life and painted the sky with exquisite hues. Amaris and the girl looked back down when a sudden splash came from the hole. The father had come back up above the water's surface. He was holding the little girl in his arms. Finally, the faint sound of sirens in the distance could be heard.

Amaris walked toward the family as they tended to the girl. As he came within ten feet, the older sister noticed him and froze in place.

"Khalah," Amaris said to the older sister as he walked past her.

As he ventured further away from the family, Amaris opened a portal and disappeared. The girl stood on the ice, astonished that he had vanished into nothingness.

يقون

Chapter Two

Resurrections

June 14, 2025

Streaks of purple light splashed like a fountain of raging water against the stone walls of the all-but-forgotten cave. Amaris stepped out of his portal. His boots stirred up the thin layer of dust that had settled onto the ground since his last visit to this place. As the portal snapped shut, the cavern returned to near-complete darkness. Amaris activated the power of Light and a small orb of white illuminated the space.

"I've come back for you," Amaris said aloud as he walked to the end of the room. "Just as I promised I would."

As he knelt down next to the forcefield surrounding Kali's still body, Amaris drew in a long sigh. He placed his hand against the flickering translucent field and it dissolved into the cool damp air of the cave.

"It was a long and mentally taxing road to get here, but I will finally have you back," Amaris said as if Kali could hear him. He placed his palm on her chest and concentrated his powers. "I'm sorry Mother, but this part is going to hurt. Istatim Halvus."

As Amaris finished chanting the spell, his hand began to glow. Kali's body reacted almost immediately. Faint twitches and tremors reverberated throughout her muscles until her eyes finally opened. Amaris looked down at her abdomen and observed that her wound had begun to bleed profusely once again.

"Who are you? Where am I?" Kali struggled to ask in between pain-induced screams that echoed throughout the cave.

"I will tell you in due time," Amaris said as he ran his hand through Kali's blood-soaked hair. "Unfortunately, right now you must die. Please try to just relax and let everything slip away."

Kali's survival instincts kicked in. She grabbed Amaris' arm and attempted to pull herself up, to no avail. With each movement, she felt waves of pain that nearly overtook her consciousness. She could feel the warmth of blood flowing freely from her body. The wound pulsated with each beat of her heart and Kali could sense that those beats were growing weaker with each moment that passed. Her eyelids began to flutter as darkness invaded the edges of her vision. She feebly grasped Amaris' arm once again… using her last ounces of strength before her heartbeat stopped and her breathing ceased.

"Qiyama Pallordium," Amaris uttered as he placed both hands on Kali's chest.

The effects were not as immediate as with Amaris' prior spell. He waited anxiously for any sign that all his efforts were not in vain. After a minute, Kali's eyes sprung wide open and she drew in an enormous gasp of air. Her weak grasp on Amaris' arm tightened like a vice as she felt a surge of energy flow through her body.

"Who are you?" she asked again when her breathing finally normalized. "What just happened to me? I felt myself die. I was gone."

"Don't worry, Mother," Amaris replied. "I am your son. I've brought you back. I am here to right the wrongs that were done to you."

"My son?" Kali asked, her voice still rough.

"Here, I will show you," Amaris replied as he held his palm against Kali's forehead and used Ane'illuminus to push his thoughts and memories into her mind.

"You're mine and Hayden's child?" Kali asked as she received the flood of information in her mind. "...and part Alva'ci?"

"Yes," he confirmed. "Hayden was wrong to hurt you. He left you here on this forgotten planet and went on with his life as if you never existed. He was all too eager to banish any thought of you in favor of that girl, Elle. Hayden needs to pay for what he did to you and so does his family."

"His family?" Kali said as she thought back to the past through the fogginess of her mind. "I remember... he was having a baby with that girl."

"He did have a baby with that girl," Amaris corrected. "Her name is Kiera. She is back at my compound on Earth."

"You captured her?" Kali asked, all the new information still not fully processed through her brain yet. "Hayden won't like that."

"Not exactly," Amaris replied. "I pushed thoughts into her mind when she was just a baby. Hayden aged her up to help him fight me... but those thoughts took root deep inside her psyche nevertheless. Now I am using her own powers of Ane'illuminus against her. She believes that she is in love with me."

"You are waging war against Hayden?" Kali asked. "I

understand your anger and frustration at what occurred, but he really had no choice. I pushed him to the edge. I took so much from him. I destroyed so many things."

"Mother, your mind and resolve have grown weak," Amaris countered. "I understand that your thinking may be clouded after you lost most of the Alva'ci's power within you. I will remedy that now, Amira."

"Amira?" Kali said, a memory from her childhood leaping into the forefront of her mind. "That was you back in Grand Marais when I was just a little girl?"

"Indeed, that was me," Amaris replied.

"How long have I been out? How old are you?" Kali wondered aloud.

"It's only been twenty-three months since Hayden put you into suspended animation," Amaris replied. "It will all become clearer to you once your mind catches up with all this new information. The pod on the Alva'ci ship sped up my development, so I appear much older than I *technically* am."

"The memories you pushed into my mind are starting to clear up now," Kali said as she attempted to stand up. "The Alva'ci genetically engineered you from my and Hayden's DNA and then added its own to the mix. So, what exactly is your plan? Revenge on my behalf? What if I don't want that? Even if I did, how in the world would I help you?"

"You lost almost all of your powers when you nearly died," Amaris replied as he placed his hand on Kali's shoulder. "I will give you access to those powers again. You will be able to feed off of my powers."

"How can I do that?" Kali asked.

"Hold still and brace yourself. There may be some pain," Amaris said before chanting a spell. "E'it ad'a layasivu."

An intense white light radiated from Amaris' palm into Kali's shoulder. She flinched as the feeling of rising power coursed through her body. A glint of orange washed over her pupils. Kali let out a long sigh and examined her body.

"Take me somewhere that I can wash up and get all this blood off me," Kali told Amaris. "What is the next step in your plan after this?"

"Right away, Mother," Amaris said as he opened a portal in front of them. "The next step… that is simple. The next step is Khalah."

ᏬᎦ ᏬᎦ ᏬᎦ ᏬᎦ ᏬᎦ ᏬᎦ

December 31, 2022
Orange County

Kali followed Amaris through a portal and stepped onto a grassy field near a large fountain. Mother and son crouched down near the marble pillars surrounding the fountain's perimeter and watched the events unfolding in the distance. Hayden was standing near a gravestone with a stone in his hand that began shining with an intense white light. He placed the stone atop the headstone and departed from the graveyard.

"Why don't you just get your revenge now?" Kali asked. "He's right there and you would catch him off-guard."

"That would change the past, Mother," Amaris replied. "There are some things you can change and get away with… and other things that would have such a profound effect that they'd completely alter the future. I cannot kill Hayden now… in this time. If I did, he wouldn't come to rescue you and defeat the Alva'ci. The creature might have never let me out of that pod. It would have almost certainly killed you to get your powers. Then it probably would have destroyed the entire planet."

"Makes sense," Kali admitted. "Too many unknowns and what-ifs."

"Exactly," Amaris said. "There is one thing that we can change here though."

"What's that?" Kali asked, intrigued.

"Follow me," Amaris replied as he rose to his feet and walked through the grass. "Hayden is gone now. It's time for the next step."

"This is my sister's grave," Kali said astonished as they stopped in front of the headstone. "Now I know why this place looked familiar. Hayden was visiting Paige's grave."

"Yes, and now that he is gone we can do what we need to," Amaris said.

"What exactly are we doing?" Kali asked.

"Watch and see," Amaris instructed.

Kali took a moment to read the etchings in her sister's headstone as Amaris repositioned himself. When she looked back at him, she noticed that the back of his right hand was glowing with the symbol of Earth. The ground beneath them started to rumble and the soil at Paige's gravesite shifted. The symbol of Air appeared on Amaris' other hand and he lifted the six feet of dirt from around Paige's coffin into the sky. Amaris closed his fist and the symbol of Air intensified as the coffin rose out of the hole. Amaris let the coffin down nearby and used his powers to place the suspended clump of soil back into the ground.

"There we are," Amaris said proudly. "You'll enjoy it much better on this side of the dirt, Khalah."

"What are you doing?" Kali asked as Amaris cracked

open the lid of Paige's coffin.

"She looks peaceful," Amaris said. "Which is ironic, because the way she died was anything but peaceful."

"Yeah, she does look as if all her troubles are gone," Kali agreed. "She's wearing one of her favorite dresses. She always looked so good in that dress."

"She does indeed," Amaris agreed as he looked over Paige's motionless body. "Okay, time for the last step."

Amaris placed his hand on Paige's chest and closed his eyes. His breathing became deeper and more focused. Kali noticed that the air around the gravesite became eerily still. The birds that had been singing in the treetops just moments ago had fallen silent.

"Qiyama Pallordium," Amaris uttered and then removed his hand from Paige's body.

"Wait… you're bringing her back?" Kali asked. She had pretty much figured that this was Amaris' plan, but now that it was actually happening, the reality of it all sank in at once.

The color of Paige's skin began to slowly change. Amaris placed two fingers on Paige's neck, waiting for the first sign of a pulse. "It's going to hurt like hell when she wakes up," he said nonchalantly. Amaris grasped his amulet and waited.

"Here we go," he finally said as Paige's body began to

twitch.

Amaris' amulet began to shine with a brilliant purple light. He placed his hand back on Paige's chest. As her eyes opened, she let out a horrifying scream. As the purple light started to pulse from Amaris' hand, time came to a standstill.

"Dammit," Kali said, as a wave of dizziness came over her.

The graveyard appeared to blur and shake visually, disorienting Kali further. Amaris strained his focus and intensified the effects of his powers. Paige's body convulsed violently as Amaris continued.

"We're almost there," Amaris yelled out over the loud humming sound that had replaced the still silence.

"I can't…" Kali stuttered before dropping to her knees and vomiting in the grass.

Amaris snickered and shook his head as Kali continued to dry heave from the visual and auditory effects of the spell. He pulled Paige's dress up to her chest to examine her torso. The puncture wounds made during the embalming process were beginning to heal and reverse. Her skin regained its normal color and her joints became relaxed. Amaris made one final push of his powers to reverse time on Paige's body.

"What the fuck was that?" Kali yelled as Amaris let off his powers and the world came back into focus for her.

"Kali?" Paige said as she opened her eyes again and sat up.

"Paige!" Kali screamed as she heard her sister's voice. She rose to her feet and walked over to Paige.

"What am I doing in this?" Paige asked in reference to the coffin that she was in. "Where are we? Is this a graveyard?"

"Paige, you were…" Kali started but was unable to finish the sentence.

"Dead," Amaris interjected. "You were dead, Khalah. Killed by the Alva'ci, or by Hayden, however you want to look at it. I brought you back."

"I remember now," Paige said as the memories came rushing back. "I remember being in Yosemite. I was in a cave and then this shadowy figure appeared. It put me on this stone table in the middle of the cave and I couldn't move. It stabbed me with a dagger. I remember at the end of it all, Hayden was there. He freed my body from the shadow's possession."

"And you died as a result," Amaris said.

"I had already died when the shadow stabbed me," Paige corrected. "My body was pretty much just a shell… a vehicle for it to travel outside the cave."

"Well, regardless, you shouldn't have died," Amaris said. "I corrected that. Now you have the opportunity to live your life."

"Wait, Kali, who is this?" Paige asked as she pointed to Amaris.

"That's a long story, sis," Kali answered. "That shadow that killed you was a spiritual manifestation of an alien creature called the Alva'ci. It tried to destroy the planet. Hayden and some others battled it and stopped it, but then it kidnapped me. The creature took me to one of its ships in space and while I was unconscious, it created a baby from mine and Hayden's DNA. Apparently, there was still some of his left inside of me from… well, you know what from. The creature mixed in its own DNA also and cooked up Amaris here in a pod."

"So, this is your son?" Paige asked astonished. "You and Hayden… and an alien?"

"Told you it was complicated," Kali said.

"Well, I'm grateful for you reviving me, Amaris," Paige said. "I remember that Hayden had powers… and there were some others like him. I assume you have the same kind of powers."

"Something like that," Amaris replied. "I am far more powerful than all of those pathetic agents of fate you killed when you were possessed. The ones that you didn't get to, your sister finished off. The only one left is Hayden."

"Were you possessed too?" Paige asked as she looked back over at Kali.

"Not exactly," Kali replied. "Remember that trip to Minnesota when we were little girls? The one where I fell into the frozen lake."

"Yeah, of course, I remember that," Paige said.

"You remember how I was somehow miraculously alive after being under the water for so long?" Kali continued. "It turns out that I also had dormant powers that ended up saving me. The Alva'ci wanted to steal those powers from me when it kidnapped me. Hayden came to save me and killed the Alva'ci, but when it died all of its power sort of exploded into a beam of energy. Most of it went into Hayden's amulet, but some of it hit me. All that power corrupted my mind."

"Oh, wow. I sure did miss a lot of stuff by being dead," Paige said as she took all the information in.

"You remember that guy that was randomly standing out on the ice after I fell in the water?" Kali asked. "He said something to you when he walked by us. That was Amaris. He can travel through time."

"What did you say to me?" Paige asked Amaris, trying to recall the word.

"I said Khalah," Amaris replied. "It means aunt."

"How did you know I was your aunt?" Paige asked. "I

was only seven years old back then."

"For me, that moment happened recently," Amaris replied. "I traveled back in time to that moment a week ago. For you though, it was many years in the past."

"Help me out of here, Kali," Paige requested as she climbed out of the coffin. Once she was standing on solid ground, she turned her attention back to Amaris. "So, you brought me back just because you felt bad about me dying?"

"Our family should be together," Amaris replied. "I brought you back for several reasons."

"Okay, like what?" Paige asked almost suspiciously.

"Yeah, like I get bringing me back. I have access to using the powers," Kali added. "But why bring Paige back... other than to give me my sister back? She doesn't have powers."

"I am building a kingdom," Amaris said. "Mother, you and I are among the powerful. Our bloodline should rule over this planet. It's only natural and right."

Okay, that sounds a little *mad dictator*, but I'll play along," Paige said. "That still doesn't explain my role in this."

"A kingdom needs rulers," Amaris said flatly. "Obviously, I will rule while I am alive... but even I cannot live forever. I need an heir."

"An heir?" Paige exclaimed, realizing Amaris' intent.

"You're plan for me, your *aunt,* is to have your children?"

"A pure bloodline is best to preserve the strength of the powers in the next generations," Amaris replied. "You are a natural choice."

"Okay, well thank you for the whole bringing me back from the dead thing," Paige said, the shock and aversion apparent in her voice. "But I think I'm going to have to pass on having kids with you. That is definitely not my vibe."

"Oh Paige, you act like I'm leaving that decision up to you," Amaris said mockingly.

Paige looked at Amaris defensively and then attempted to back away from him. He grabbed her by the arm and pulled her closer, while she struggled to get away. Amaris placed his other hand on her forehead and closed his eyes in focus.

"You will do whatever I ask of you," Amaris said, his voice now echoing in several octaves at once as he pushed the command into Paige's mind.

"I will do anything you ask me to," Paige replied obediently.

"Amaris!" Kali yelled. "That is not…"

"Quiet, Mother," Amaris barked. "Do not make me do the same thing to you. While you may have powers, you are no match for me."

Kali's resultant sigh relayed her disdain, but also her surrender. Amaris let go of Paige's arm and turned his attention to cleaning up the evidence of their presence in the graveyard. Symbols of power lit on both of his hands. The coffin previously housing Paige rose into the air and then Amaris hit it with a stream of Fire. The ashes floated away in the breeze and erased the last indicator they had been there.

"Let's go," Amaris said as he opened a new portal.

غادريل

Chapter Three

Khalah

2049 - Los Angeles

Amaris led Kali and Paige out of the portal into a large warehouse. Sections of the room were partitioned off with drapes. In the background were the sounds of various machines humming and beeping in a constant rhythm.

"Welcome to my base of operations," Amaris said to the sisters. "Hayden destroyed my last one, so I found this place. I must say that it is quite the upgrade from what I had before."

"Base of operations for what?" Kali asked.

"Preparing to go back and take over," Amaris said as he pulled a drape open and revealed a dozen hospital-style gurneys, each with an unconscious woman strapped to it. "There are several more sections of the warehouse like this."

"Holy shit," Kali said as she walked through the area observing the women. "Why do you have all these people here?"

"These unfortunate wanderers of the wasteland are being given a great gift," Amaris replied smugly. "Their previously meaningless lives will now have a point. They will provide me with an army."

"An army?" Kali asked, putting more pieces of the puzzle together in her mind. "I take it that they are not your army themselves."

"No," Amaris said with a chuckle. "Over the past couple of weeks, I captured every girl and woman I could find within her fertile years. They will *provide* me with the army."

"Wait, there's a dozen women here and you said there are several more sections like this?" Kali asked.

"Yes," Amaris replied as he walked along the draped areas of the warehouse and pulled the curtains to each section open. "There are a total of nine sections, each with a dozen occupants. Turns out that these people are really easy to catch."

"You can't possibly be thinking that you're going to be able to have children with all of them," Kali said perplexed.

"Like, time-wise and physically… that would be insane. Also, some of these women are twice your age… and others are years younger than you."

"Relax, Mother. I have no desire to engage in the physical process with any of these subjects," Amaris replied as he led Kali and Paige into another area of the warehouse with several machines and tables full of medical equipment. "I am going to extract eggs from each of the subjects and use the lab to create embryos using my DNA."

"So, an army of children… of infants?" Kali asked.

"This is the key," Amaris said as he placed his hand on a piece of equipment that differed in appearance from everything else in the room. "I went back to the Alva'ci's ship and recovered the pod that I was kept in. I examined it and I was able to build several more pods just like it. Once the embryos are made, the pods will speed their physical development up. I will have an army of fully-grown soldiers in a matter of weeks."

"Amaris?" a girl's voice called out from just outside the room. "Are you back?"

"Kiera," Amaris replied as she appeared in the doorway. "Yes, I am back. I have brought my mother Kali and her sister Paige with me. How are you, darling?"

"I'm good," Kiera said as she kissed Amaris on the

cheek, then turned to face the sisters. "I'm pleased to meet both of you."

"It's good to meet you, Kiera," Kali said. "Do you know who I am?"

"Yes, I know all about you," Kiera replied. "My father and I discussed who you were… or *are*."

"I guess I'm surprised by you," Kali said to Amaris. "That you aren't using Kiera to produce your heir."

"I've considered it," Amaris admitted. "I would rather keep the bloodline pure within our family, if possible. However, if Paige fails to conceive before the war begins, then I will enlist Kiera in the task instead. For the moment though, just her presence here provides me with leverage."

"Do you want to show Kali and Paige their rooms?" Kiera asked.

"Excellent idea," Amaris said as he started leading everyone out of the room and up a staircase.

Upon reaching the second floor, the group walked down a long hallway until they came to several rooms converted into residences. On either side of the hallway were a set of doors. Amaris opened the first door on the left.

"This is my room," he said. "The next door there is Kiera's room. Now, in here is your room, Mother."

The first door on the right side of the hallway

contained a spacious area, complete with a bed, vanity, sofa, kitchenette, and a restroom.

"Wow, this is actually really nice," Kali said.

"Thank you. I put a lot of effort into making sure this was a comfortable space for everyone," Amaris replied. He walked over to the next door and opened it, revealing a similarly appointed room. "Paige, this is your room."

Paige walked inside the room and looked around. Amaris, Kali, and Kiera followed her inside. Paige opened the closet door and found an assortment of clothes all in her sizes.

"Wow, this is so nice," Paige said.

"Well, now that everyone knows their living arrangements, there is work that needs to begin. In fact, there is a long list of things to accomplish in a relatively short amount of time," Amaris said to the group. "Forgive me for being blunt and rushing things. We will have time to rest later. First, Paige, remove your clothes and take a shower. When you are finished, wait for me on your bed."

"Paige, geez…" Kali said surprised when her sister immediately obeyed Amaris' command and stripped nude in front of everyone.

"Kiera, please take my mother back down to the lab and show her how things work," Amaris continued his instructions. "Once Paige and I finish, we will join you."

Kali's face flashed a look of disapproval, knowing what Amaris was about to do with her sister. However, she also knew that her son could easily kill her... and that he might be crazy enough to do so. Kali conceded her thoughts on the matter and followed Kiera down the hallway.

Forty-five minutes later, Amaris appeared in the lab with Paige at his side. "How are things faring down here?" he asked.

"So what is the plan now?" Kali asked. "Remain here, create an army, and then wage war?"

"Before we proceed on that route, I will give Hayden one chance," Amaris said. "Tomorrow, I will go to the past and talk to him. My plan was to eliminate him long before I resurrected you and Paige. I have the two of you back now. In an effort to appease you, Mother, I will offer Hayden a truce. If he stays out of my way in taking over the planet, then I will let him and Elle live. He must accept my terms though."

"You actually think he will agree to that?" Kali asked sarcastically.

"It is unlikely," Amaris admitted. "But I am willing to make the offer... for you. If he accepts, then we can forgo creating the army. I won't need an army if Hayden doesn't get in my way."

"If he refuses?" Paige asked.

"Then when I return here, we will proceed with the first round of egg extractions and make sure that these pods are working correctly. After I am satisfied with the army's size and strength, we will travel back in time and take over the world by force. Hayden will meet the same fate as anyone else who stands in our way."

ⳤ ⳤ ⳤ ⳤ ⳤ ⳤ

The next morning, Kali and Paige woke and readied themselves before heading down to the warehouse. When they arrived downstairs, they found Amaris and Kiera in the lab working on the equipment.

"How did you two sleep?" Amaris asked.

"Very well," Paige replied.

"Not too bad," Kali added.

"Well, if there is anything that I can do to make either of you more comfortable, just let me know," Amaris said. "Kiera and I are just finishing up here. You're just in time to see me depart for the past."

"Good luck, darling," Kiera told Amaris. "Tell my mother and father that I say hello."

"I will," Amaris said as he opened a portal. "Please keep Kali and Paige company. I won't be gone for too long."

June 15, 2025
Camarillo, California

Dan stood at the edge of the concrete and grass beside Hayden and Elle's pool, readying himself to dive in. Hayden and Abby waited inside the pool to watch. Elle stood in the kitchen, pouring herself a glass of water and watching through the window. She made her way outside before Dan had even finished hyping up his impending jump.

As Dan began to run toward the edge of the pool, a bright purple portal opened in the backyard. Dan's dive turned into a flailing belly-flop against the water as he freaked out at the appearance of Amaris coming through the portal. When Dan came back up above water, he saw that Hayden had already made his way to the steps to exit the pool. Dan swam over to Abby's side in a protective gesture.

"Good morning everyone," Amaris said. "I see that you all are getting along quite nicely."

"What do you want?" Hayden asked in a demanding tone. Hayden attempted to keep Amaris' attention drawn toward him since Elle was now only a few feet behind their uninvited guest.

"Well, the gang is almost all here," Amaris remarked before looking over his shoulder. "Oh, there you are Elle."

"Leave her alone, Amaris," Hayden insisted. "Why are you here?"

"I guess I haven't seen you quite in a while," Amaris said as he walked up to Elle, while ignoring Hayden's command. "How far along are you?"

"That's not any of your business," Elle replied.

"Aren't you feisty… I like that about you," Amaris told her. "Might I say, you look absolutely stunning pregnant."

"Amaris!" Hayden yelled as he approached from behind.

"Oh, by the way, Kiera wanted me to tell you both that she says hello," Amaris said as he turned back to face Hayden.

The back of Hayden's right hand began to glow intensely with the symbol of Fire. "One last chance. What do you want?"

"I have come to offer you a truce," Amaris said, the amusement in his voice evident. "I have attained what I wanted. I believed that I would have to kill you along the way, but evidently that was not necessary. So, I offer an olive branch."

"Peace?" Hayden replied suspiciously. "You have my

daughter under your control. Why in the world would I agree to a truce without her here."

"You can have her back," Amaris said. "If you agree to my terms."

"This ought to be good," Hayden said. "What would those be?"

"Simple," Amaris said. "You stay out of my way and I let everyone here live… and I'll give Kiera back."

"Out of your way for what, exactly?" Elle chimed in.

"Making this world a better place," Amaris replied. "I intend to rule over every nation on this planet. Our bloodline is the most powerful force that this universe has ever known. We are meant to rule. As I'm sure Hayden knows from his encounter with Bilv'at, we have the capacity to be near immortal. To have lives that span thousands of years. Just think of what could be accomplished. All that I request is that Hayden stays out of my way and does not challenge or attack me. In return, I will let you all live in peace in the new world."

"What's the alternative?" Hayden asked.

"Well, the alternative is that I come back and take the world by force," Amaris replied. "The end result is the same. I still end up ruling, but all of you are dead. Actually, I might keep Elle alive. I am a little fond of her."

"What I wonder, Amaris, is why you thought I would

ever agree to this?" Hayden asked. "You think that I'd trust you to keep your word? You think I would just let you become some evil world dictator and just look the other way because my family was safe."

"Think about it," Amaris replied. "It's your family and friends that you care about. All of those people out there in the world, they don't mean anything to you. Sure, you sit here and object to me ruling because of some faux sense of nobility and moral superiority. At the end of the day, you would let the world burn if it meant saving your family. This truce would have you all live in peace, for a very long time. You know the spell to achieve that. Bilv'at taught me the same spell that she taught those villagers thousands of years ago. I know she taught it to you too, because she told me that she did."

"The world you propose is not one that I would want my kids to live in. It's not one that I would want Elle to endure," Hayden said. "Your notion of a perfect world is ill conceived. I won't agree to it, I can't."

"Very well," Amaris said as he opened another portal, preparing to leave. "I figured that I would try. For my mother's sake. We will all see you again soon… but not with tidings of peace."

"That Bilv'at lady taught you an immortality spell?"

Dan asked after Amaris disappeared into his portal.

"The spell that she apparently taught Amaris is not the same one she taught me," Hayden replied. "I could tell by the way he explained it. He learned a much weaker version. I don't think that he knows that Bilv'at lied to him about what she taught me."

"Okay, still, an immortality spell," Elle interrupted. "No matter how strong or weak, you wouldn't seriously use that… right?"

"I don't know," Hayden admitted. "I haven't given it any serious thought. I can't say that I'm diametrically opposed to the concept of actually spending *forever* with you."

"Okay, when you put it that way it's different," Elle said. "But still, don't you think that is way too long to live? What happens in a thousand years when you've done everything you could possibly imagine and you're bored of existence?"

"Well, sign me up," Dan interjected. "If I get bored, then I'll just take a six year nap on the piles of cash that I accumulated over the years."

"If you had thousands of years, you could be a constant figure for good and stability in the world," Hayden added. "In case other people like Amaris come along. The people of the world cannot fight that kind of power alone."

"Is that really your responsibility though?" Elle asked.

"That's a good question," Hayden admitted. "Just because I fulfilled some prophecy doesn't mean that I must dedicate my life to keeping the world safe. I would much rather spend my time with my family."

"Either way, it doesn't look like we are going to get a normal life until after Amaris is defeated," Elle said.

"I agree," Hayden said. "Let's hope that after he is dealt with, we can have some lasting peace."

～ ～ ～ ～ ～ ～

2049 - Los Angeles

Amaris reappeared in the warehouse. He walked down to the lab area and found Kiera teaching Kali and Paige about the conditions in the wasteland outside the warehouse.

"As you predicted, Hayden declined my offer," Amaris said to Kali. "We will proceed with the plan."

"Very well," Kiera said. "I am ready when you are."

"Let's begin now," Amaris said. "Kali and Paige can observe how this all works in real life instead of just theory."

Kiera and Amaris prepared themselves for the procedure and then led Kali and Paige into the first draped-off section of the warehouse. As Amaris retrieved a large needle and attached it to a suction device via catheter, Kiera stood at the side of the first bed and recited subject information.

"The first section houses twelve subjects," Kiera said. "Subject names are unknown. For procedure purposes, they will be referred to as numbers one through twelve. Each subject will be undergoing oocyte retrieval."

"Very good. Carry one," Amaris said to Kiera as he turned on the ultrasound machine.

"Subjects one through six are as follows," Kiera continued as she read off a stack of charts:

"Subject one, a twenty-seven-year-old female, stable.

Subject two, a twenty-one-year-old female, stable.

Subject three, a thirty-two-year-old female, stable.

Subject four, a fifteen-year-old female, stable.

Subject five, a nineteen-year-old female, stable.

Subject six, a twenty-four-year-old female, slightly

low sats, BP is currently stable."

"Great, let's proceed," Amaris said to Kiera as he handed her the ultrasound probe. "After this group of subjects, you can continue on your own."

Kiera positioned the first subject and Amaris began the procedure. After using the ultrasound to locate the follicles, he inserted the needle and extracted just over a dozen eggs. Kiera took the samples back to the lab while Amaris prepared the next subject. Three hours later, the procedure had been completed on the first group of twelve subjects.

"Alright, based on the normal calculations, we should have up to a hundred and ninety-eight new soldiers for our army," Amaris said. "I don't know about the rest of you, but I am hungry now. After we have lunch, Kiera can continue on in the lab with the fertilization, preservation, and development stages. Kali, I would like you to observe her and learn how you can help. Paige, you and I will meet in your room again."

"How quickly will this army be ready?" Kali asked as she sat down at the table in the makeshift dining room area.

"With the twenty development pods that we have here, set on the maximum settings, we can finish eighty soldiers in a day," Amaris replied. "We will do another egg extraction on all of the subjects in twenty-eight days and produce another batch of soldiers. Sixty days from now, we should have an army of approximately four thousand. Then we will attack."

"So, sixty days in this warehouse," Kali said.

"Yes," Amaris replied. "You should use the time to learn from Kiera and to practice using your powers again.

You haven't attempted it once since I revived you."

"Perhaps I don't want to," Kali retorted.

"I don't care if you want to," Amaris said. "We must be unified in this effort. You will be there at the battle. If you don't attempt to practice on your own volition, then I will have Kiera attack you so you're forced to defend yourself."

Kali didn't answer Amaris' threat but instead began eating the lunch that Kiera had placed on the table. Amaris followed suit, assuming that his message had been received loud and clear. The remainder of the meal passed in silence.

"Let's go, Paige," Amaris instructed once she finished her meal."

෴ ෴ ෴ ෴ ෴ ෴

Twenty-Two Days Later

Amaris woke at six o'clock in the morning and showered in preparation for another day full of lab work. As he exited his bedroom, Paige opened her door and greeted him.

"Look at this," she said as she held out the pregnancy test that she had just taken.

While on one of his excursions into the past, Amaris had obtained a large box of tests to be ready for this phase of his plan. He required Paige to take a test every three days.

"Positive," he replied as he looked down at the test. "That is excellent news. Let's head down to the lab and we can inform the others once they join us."

Paige accompanied Amaris to the lab where they began the daily task of placing new embryos into the development pods. After starting the first batch, they heard footsteps in the hallway indicating that Kali and Kiera had made their way downstairs.

"Breakfast?" Amaris asked Kiera as he entered the kitchen area with Paige.

"Coming right up," Kiera replied as she set a plate down on the table at Amaris' spot.

Kali shoveled bites of food into her mouth in an effort to avoid any conversation. She had begrudgingly begun training with her powers again, mostly because she was afraid of what Amaris would do to her if she disobeyed him. However, each time that she used a power, she also felt a surge of the corruption that had once taken over her mind. She made every effort to resist it while still appearing to be compliant.

"Paige, don't you have some news that you would like to share with everyone?" Amaris asked.

"I'm pregnant!" Paige declared to the group.

Kali spit her breakfast back into her bowl and just barely managed to hold back an involuntary surge of vomit. Kiera got up from her seat and congratulated Paige, as if she hadn't even noticed Kali's reaction.

"Is there a problem?" Amaris snarled at Kali.

"Just the fact that you impregnated my sister," Kali replied as she continued to attempt holding down her breakfast. "My sister… your aunt!"

"Stop being insolent, Mother," Amaris rebuked. "Paige is delighted with this development."

"She's delighted?" Kali challenged. "You're in control of her thoughts! Of course she's delighted… because you're making her feel that way."

"Are we going to have a problem?" Amaris asked menacingly. "I was under the impression that you were strong, formidable, and ruthless. All I see is a weak woman who is hellbent on forgiving the person that almost killed her. A woman who is completely ungrateful for the gift of life that her son gave to her."

"We are going to have a problem," Kali replied. "Let me take my sister out of here… back to the past. We don't need to be a part of this scheme of yours."

"Silence!" Amaris demanded.

Kali stood up from her place at the table. A

momentary flicker of orange danced around her pupils. Amaris rose slowly and stared her down. Kali's palms ignited with Fire as she prepared herself for what would almost certainly be imminent death. Kiera's attention turned away from Paige and she thrust her palm toward Kali, who immediately flew back against the wall of the kitchen area. Amaris walked up to his mother and took one of her hands in his. A symbol of power illuminated on his hand and the Fire in Kali's palms died out. With his other hand, he gripped Kali's throat.

"If you attempt to stand against me again," Amaris began. "I will either kill you myself… or if I am feeling sentimental, then I will strap you to a gurney and you'll become another piece of human livestock to provide me with an army."

"You wouldn't," Kali said in shock through gasps for air.

"Try me," Amaris replied in a stone-cold voice before releasing Kali's throat and letting her fall to the ground.

"Get up and congratulate your sister," Amaris instructed Kali.

"Congratulations," Kali said to Paige as she walked over and sat next to her sister, though the look in Kali's eyes sent a message that conflicted with her words.

"Are you excited to be an aunt?" Paige asked.

"Yeah, of course sis," Kali replied as she caught Amaris still glaring at her.

"Well, I'm excited to have a little niece or nephew," Kiera chimed in.

"If you'll all excuse me, I am going to go practice with my powers," Kali said as she walked away from the table.

"I bet you are," Amaris replied. "Tread very carefully."

ᔕ ᔕ ᔕ ᔕ ᔕ ᔕ

July 8, 2025
Fullerton, California

"This soup is so good," Abby said in between shoving spoonfuls of it in her mouth. "Where did you learn about this place?"

"Some guy in one of my classes," Dan replied. "His brother just opened the place last month. I've been meaning to come here, so I figured we could try it together."

"This might become a new place on the short-list," Abby declared. "I'll wait until we get the main course though before I decide."

"So are you ready to join all of us down in Irvine?"

Dan asked in reference to Abby's recent graduation from Cal State Fullerton. She was one year behind Dan and Hayden.

"I am more than ready," Abby said. "Not having all of you around here to hang out with in between classes sucks."

"Well, now you get the benefit of us knowing where everything is at Irvine," Dan replied. "You won't have to wander around and find things like we did."

"You're still probably going to have to walk me to my classes for like the entire first week," Abby joked.

"You won't hear me complaining about that," Dan replied.

"Oh, that looks delicious," Abby said as the server brought out the main course.

"Just wait until you taste it," Dan replied through a half chewed bite.

After the meal, Abby veered off course from their path to the car. A small park next to the shopping center that housed the new restaurant had caught her eye. She frolicked along the sidewalk toward the gate. Dan followed and chuckled to himself as he thought about how happy Abby seemed. Knowing the point in her life she had come from just six months prior, it brought him joy to see Abby in such a good place.

"Swing with me!" Abby yelled to Dan as she sat down

on one of the two seats on the swingset.

Dan obeyed her command and the duo engaged in a friendly battle to see who could swing higher. Eventually, Abby leapt from her seat and tumbled into the grass in front of them. Dan walked to her and sat by her side.

"Hey Dan," Abby started.

"What's up?" he asked.

"Thank you for being around so much over the past few months," she replied.

"Of course. I love hanging out with you," Dan said.

"I know you've probably been waiting on an answer," Abby stated.

"That's not why I've been around so much," Dan insisted.

"I know," Abby said. "I told you that I would think about your question. I also told you that it might take some time for me to figure out my answer. I didn't mean to keep you waiting around this long."

"You're fine," Dan replied. "There is no rush. I just enjoy being with you."

"Thanks," Abby said gratefully. "It's been on my mind a lot lately. I think that I am ready. If you still want to date me, then I'm saying yes."

"Really?" Dan said, the excitement in his voice

apparent. "Yeah, I do. I most definitely do."

"Okay then… boyfriend," Abby said. "Just promise me that you'll communicate and be open with me. I haven't been in a dating relationship in a long time, so cut me some slack."

"Of course," Dan assured her. "I promise. As long as you communicate with me too."

"You got it," Abby said before leaning over and kissing Dan on the lips.

"Well this just became my new favorite park in the whole world," Dan joked.

෧ ෧ ෧ ෧ ෧ ෧

July 8, 2025 - 10:00 p.m.
Camarillo, California

Elle reclined on the couch as she and Hayden watched a movie in the living room. His head was perched on her belly, with an ear listening for any activity from the baby while he held a sideways glance on the television screen.

"How's it going down there?" Elle asked.

"She's moving around a little bit," Hayden replied. "Probably busy plotting her imminent escape."

"I know, any day now and she'll be here," Elle agreed. "This time we are actually going to wait like a year at least before another one. I want to get my body back for a little while."

"Well, for the record, I think you look quite beautiful pregnant," Hayden replied. "But yeah, I bet you're ready for a break."

"Thank you, but yes I am definitely ready for a break," Elle said with a laugh. "Plus, with that threat from Amaris, I would rather not potentially be running for my life while pregnant."

"Running for your life?" Hayden said mockingly, as if he were offended by the suggestion. "Do you think I'm going to let things get so out of control that you have to run and hide?"

"No, but I'm just saying," Elle replied. "Better safe than sorry."

"Speaking of that, I think I am going to go into the dreamscape tonight and consult with the orb," Hayden said. "I've been thinking about the best way to defeat Amaris, but some out of the box ideas would be good."

"That is true," Elle agreed. "We have no idea when he will be back. Anything that can be done to get Kiera back safely is okay in my book."

———

Hayden continued to watch the rest of the movie with Elle before they retired to the bedroom. She fell asleep effortlessly and Hayden decided to use the time alone to head into the dreamscape. As he awoke inside, the orb answered his call and appeared in front of him.

"What brings you here?" the orb asked.

"Amaris," Hayden replied. "I would like your opinion on the easiest way to defeat him without a huge loss of life. The last time we fought, he was a difficult opponent. I imagine that he is even stronger now. He has my daughter as a captive. I don't want anything to happen to her... and I have another daughter on the way."

"You don't want to destroy the world in the process of saving it," the orb paraphrased Hayden's words back to him.

"Exactly," Hayden agreed. "I want a world for my wife and girls to live peacefully in."

"Peace is a fleeting thing," the orb said.

"Seems so," Hayden said. "Some days I would give away these powers to just live a quiet life."

"The threats would still come," the orb advised. "Maybe you wouldn't be the one fighting them... but instead you would be an innocent bystander, wholly dependent on the skills of whoever was fighting. Would you rather leave the fate of your family in someone else's hands?"

"No, I wouldn't," Hayden replied.

"Then accept your fate," the orb advised. "Dreaming of an idyllic life doesn't make it happen. You aren't some unfortunate victim of the universe. You have been given great power, so use it."

"I know. Let's focus on what I came here for," Hayden said.

"Defeating Amaris without bloodshed," the orb replied. "That might be impossible. Especially with an all out battle. The two of you could level entire cities with a drawn out fight."

"So, your suggestion?" Hayden asked.

"The powers of your descendants manifest at puberty," the orb said. "If you can obtain a moment to age Amaris down, his powers will disappear. His grasp over your daughter's mind should also vanish. The tricky part will be finding a moment amidst the battle to actually achieve this."

"True, he will not be waiting around idly," Hayden said.

"If you can knock him out or even stun him for several moments, then you will have sufficient time to cast the spell you need," the orb advised. "Until then, expect a catastrophic fight."

"Great, so the best plan is basically a what-if," Hayden

said. "Even if I can age him down, isn't that you prolonging the inevitable? He will grow up again and then we repeat the cycle ad infinitum."

"There are things you can do to prevent him from holding that grudge," the orb said.

"Erase his mind," Hayden concluded. "Age him down to a baby and wipe the slate clean."

"Exactly," the orb agreed. "Then it will be on you to raise him in a way that doesn't repeat the past."

"Okay, I can do that," Hayden declared. "I will have to do that. Thank you for your thoughts."

"Until next time," the orb said as it vanished from sight.

بينيمو

Chapter Four

Descendants of Wrath

July 10, 2025

Hayden stood by Elle's side as she rested in between contractions. The room bore a reassuring uniformity with the one they had been in for Kiera's birth. The only thing that seemed to have changed was the room number. After forty-five minutes, Elle gave birth to a baby girl.

"Kinsley," Hayden remarked as he held her in his arms. "Finally, we meet in person."

"She's not going to stay this little for long; is she?" Elle asked as Hayden handed the baby off.

"I'm afraid that she most likely won't," Hayden admitted. "From what she said in my dreams, it is probable that I will have to age her up soon."

"Okay. Well, I'm going to enjoy her being a baby while I can," Elle said. "Hayden, after all of this is finished and our lives are finally normal... can we have one more? One that can actually remain a baby and have a real childhood?"

"Yes," Hayden answered as he kissed Elle on the forehead. "As many as you want."

"French toast," Elle said.

"French... what?" Hayden asked, confused.

"What you said just now," Elle replied. "It reminded me of the morning of my fifteenth birthday party. You were making French toast. My brother was being a jerk because I asked you if you were making it for me. You said that I could have as much as I want."

"Ohhh," Hayden said as he recalled the morning that Elle was talking about. "I remember that. It was a really good morning... and that evening we spent hours on the back patio together talking and eating ice cream."

"Yeah, it was a really good day," Elle agreed.

"French toast," Hayden said, repeating her earlier phrase. "Babies and french toast, you can have as many of either as you'd like."

"Either?" Elle asked jokingly. "By either, you better mean that I can have as many as I want of both."

"Yes, both," Hayden confirmed. "Though the more babies, the more expensive the French toast bill will be."

Elle's resulting laughter startled Kinsley from her sleep. "I'm sorry baby," Elle said in a soothing voice. Kinsley appeared to immediately forgive the intrusion on her slumber and began suckling on Elle's breast.

❧ ❧ ❧ ❧ ❧ ❧

August 15, 2025

"Okay, yeah we will turn it on now," Elle said into her phone.

Elle walked down the hallway to the kitchen and found Hayden. From the look on her face, he could tell that something was wrong.

"Abby called and said to turn on the news," Elle said. "Something is happening in Los Angeles."

"Has the day finally come?" Hayden asked aloud as he flicked on the television.

"A strange occurrence, happening right now in Los Angeles," the news anchor said. A split-screen view of helicopter footage showed the scene. "A large vortex-like anomaly appeared just minutes ago in the middle of the intersection at South Olive Street and Fourth Street in the downtown area. People seem to be coming out of the anomaly… hundreds of people so far. They are filling the streets. The scene is chaotic. Police have yet to arrive on the scene, but a spokesperson for the LAPD has communicated that anyone in the area should leave if it is safe to do so. If you were headed to the downtown area, you should cancel your trip until the situation has been resolved. Metro subway lines that run through downtown have been halted. We will keep an eye on this as events unfold."

"That's Amaris right there," Hayden said when the helicopter camera zoomed in closer.

"Where did he get all of those people? It's like an army," Elle said.

"Wait, is that… and…" Hayden stuttered.

"Who?" Elle asked.

"It is," Hayden replied and pointed at the screen. "Kiera is right there, about twenty feet away from Amaris. Kali and Paige are standing next to her."

"Kali?" Elle said with a gasp. "How are those two there?"

"Bilv'at must have taught him the spell of resurrection," Hayden said grimly. "She taught it to me also."

"He can bring people back from the dead?" Elle asked fearfully.

"Yes, but he has to be touching the person to cast the spell," Hayden replied. "It's not like he can bring back a horde of people in one fell swoop."

"Still, that is insane," Elle said. "I understand why Kali is there with him, she was crazy. But her sister… why is she there? You said she was a good friend of yours."

"I am sure that he has her under his control, just like with Kiera," Hayden answered. "Now is the moment when I can try to break that control. Now we can get Kiera back."

Hayden grabbed his phone and called Armond. After a brief conversation, Hayden took Elle and Kinsley with him through a portal to Armond's home.

"Dan and I will accompany you to the scene," Armond said as everyone arrived. "We may not be much help, but we will do what we can."

"Okay, just try not to die," Hayden advised. "Elle and Abby can go back to our house with the baby. I will try to defeat Amaris on my own. If I cannot do that, I will come back for Kinsley."

"Be safe, babe," Elle pleaded as she kissed him.

"I will," Hayden replied. "Be back soon, one way or the other."

Hayden opened a set of portals. Elle and Abby took Kinsley through the one destined for Camarillo, while

Hayden accompanied Armond and Dan through the second portal to Los Angeles.

ↄ ↄ ↄ ↄ ↄ ↄ

With a flash of orange light, Hayden's portal opened in downtown at the corner of Olive and Fifth. A block away, Amaris' portal was still open and spewing forth a seemingly endless stream of soldiers. Hayden spotted Amaris standing atop the terrace adjacent to California Plaza Park. The growing army filled the streets. Amaris shouted an order to attack, and a large group of soldiers rushed toward Hayden, Armond, and Dan.

"Just try and stand your ground," Hayden said to Armond and Dan as he brought up forcefields around them. "These fields will protect you, but they won't last forever. Also, a Chantiatus forcefield is really good against projectiles or power-based attacks, but if someone gets in close enough to engage in a fist-fight with you then the blows will land. It may not hurt as much when you get punched or kicked, but if you encounter sustained attacks you will begin to feel it."

The first wave of soldiers arrived within striking distance, and Hayden let out a blast of energy that sent them flying backwards through the air. A second and third wave approached, ending in much the same fashion. As the groups of soldiers became larger, some of them were able to slip through.

"Here we go!" Dan shouted to Armond as a small group of attacks slipped by Hayden and came toward them.

As the two men engaged in a hand-to-hand brawl with their opponents, Hayden continued using his powers to neutralize large groups at a time. Everyone's attention was drawn upwards as the sound of shattering glass echoed through the streets. A few seconds later, shards of glass fell from the sky accompanied by office furniture and other debris. Some members of Amaris' army had infiltrated surrounding buildings and were mounting a quasi aerial assault. Smoke started billowing from the windows of other nearby buildings as the soldiers lit fires to create a chaotic environment.

"You okay?" Hayden shouted back to Dan and Armond.

"Maybe!" Dan yelled back. His voice didn't instill much confidence in Hayden's mind.

"Geez!" Hayden said as he turned around to see two soldiers holding Armond while another was punching him repeatedly. Dan was attempting to intervene, unsuccessfully, and was being beaten from behind by another soldier. "Ask me for help if you need it."

"We would've managed," Dan said after Hayden electrocuted the two soldiers and sent several other nearby attackers flying with a pulse of energy.

"You know who Abby is going to be mad at if you get the crap pummeled out of you?" Hayden asked. "Me… she'll be mad at me. I don't feel like being the bad guy here, so try not to get your ass kicked, please."

"Thank you for your help," Armond said as he brushed the dust from his clothes.

"You should know better," Hayden chided his mentor. "With all the times you've told me not to be reckless."

"You were a little preoccupied," Armond said.

"Okay, they're going to just keep coming until we're overwhelmed," Hayden said as more soldiers rounded the corner. "We need to get up there and get Kiera back."

Hayden opened a portal and the trio teleported up to the terrace. They stepped out only a few paces away from Amaris, Kali, Paige, and Kiera.

"Did you really have to step in there, Hayden?" Amaris asked. "I was going to enjoy watching those two get beaten to death."

"I'm not here to play around," Hayden replied. "I want my daughter back and I'm going to do whatever it takes to accomplish that."

"Hayden," Kali uttered, but was unable to formulate a sentence after calling out his name.

"Is that actually you?" Hayden asked cautiously.

"It is," she replied. "I'm not here to fight you, but he has Kiera and Paige under his control."

"Mother, what did I tell you about crossing me?" Amaris said as a Flame ignited in his palm.

Kali fired a stream of energy at Amaris, which he held at bay. He used his other hand to send a stream of Fire in her direction. Mother and son went back and forth, fighting amongst themselves.

"Kiera," Hayden pushed his thoughts into her head while Amaris was distracted. "Break yourself from Amaris' control and come to me."

"Stay out of my head!" she pushed back and sent a pulse of energy toward Hayden.

Hayden deflected Kiera's attack and concluded that the Alva'ci had been correct. Amaris' control over her mind would only be broken if he were either killed or aged down. Hayden glanced over at Kali and Amaris to make sure that they were still occupied with each other and then turned his attention to Paige. He hoped that his control over her was weaker, since she had no powers to use against herself.

"Paige, can you hear me?" Hayden asked as he pushed

the thought into her mind. "Amaris is using you. He is controlling you. Be free of him. I command you to be free."

Paige's eyes darted back and forth as she looked at the cityscape like she'd never seen it before. She shook her head as if coming out of a foggy daze. Her hand lowered to her stomach. As she held it there and appeared lost in thought, she began to cry.

"Hayden, please help me," Paige cried out.

Amaris and Kali both halted their attacks against each other as they heard Paige speak. Amaris began walking toward her.

"Go hide somewhere!" Hayden yelled to Paige as he pointed both palms at Amaris.

An enormous column of infused Light and Darkness shot from Hayden's hands and rocketed toward Amaris. As he withstood the brunt of the attack for several seconds, Paige took the opportunity to run. Once she was out of sight, Hayden ended the attack.

"You are seriously annoying me," Amaris said to Hayden. "Now I'm going to have to punish her after all this is over. I'll make sure she understands that all the pain is because of you. For now, let's just focus on eliminating you."

Hayden heard a growing shriek just in time to turn around and see a cluster of fiery boulders hurtling through the air at him. He dove out of the way and the projectiles exploded against a building across the street.

"Pretty quick for an old man," Amaris joked.

"You're not quick enough," Hayden replied as a bolt of Electricity crackled from his palm and struck Amaris in the chest.

Amaris stood back up and leveled his gaze at his father, who took the cue that the battle was about to begin. Hayden renewed the forcefields around Dan and Armond and readied himself.

"Attack them!" Amaris yelled as a portal opened behind Hayden's group. A dozen soldiers streamed out and began fighting Dan and Armond.

Finally, Amaris sent a strong pulse of energy at Hayden to answer his father's attack. He deftly redirected the attack into the sky and the two began a volley of assaults against each other. After several minutes, neither had landed any meaningful blow against the other, but the damage to nearby buildings was considerable.

Kali recovered from her injuries and began sneaking toward Amaris from the rear. Hayden noticed that she looked poised to attack again. Kiera stepped toward her and shot a blast of energy at Kali, knocking her back to the ground. The sound of sirens flooded the streets as police presence finally arrived to address the situation. Hayden took the brief pause in fighting to pick off a few of the soldiers attacking Dan and Armond.

On the streets below the terrace, Amaris' army was hard at work. Some fought with the police officers as they arrived, while others continued to light fires and destroy property. The scene was looking increasingly grim.

"Soon, you'll be overwhelmed," Amaris said to Hayden. "Do you actually think that you can win against my entire force?"

"You're a little too confident, aren't you?" Hayden replied.

"I wouldn't have taken you to be so naive," Amaris said as he waved his hand over his head.

A flood of soldiers hurried up the staircase from the street to the terrace and surrounded Hayden's group. As they attacked from all sides, Amaris fired off his own barrage of attacks at Hayden. As he fought on every front, Hayden could feel the pain building from Amaris' blows landing repeatedly. He looked over toward Dan and Armond to see that they were now on the ground, curled up defensively as a circle of soldiers kicked at their bodies. Hayden let out a shockwave of energy that devastated all the soldiers on the terrace.

"More are coming to take their places," Amaris said

as he smirked. The sound of boots hurriedly ascending the staircase confirmed his words.

"This isn't over," Hayden said. He ran toward Dan and Armond, helped them to their feet, and then pushed them through a portal before following them through.

كاسداي

Chapter Five

The Future is Now

Vista Hermosa Park - Los Angeles

Hayden stood in the shade of a sycamore tree with Armond and Dan next to him. The Los Angeles skyline rose in the background. A large explosion echoed through the streets and a plume of black smoke billowed into the sky. In the distance, Amaris' army went on the offensive against the sea of police officers that had responded to the crisis.

"It is time," Hayden said. "I cannot do this alone. We need to go back to Camarillo."

"We're right behind you, buddy," Dan said as he examined the plethora of bruises covering his torso.

Hayden opened a portal and the three of them walked

through. They exited on the other side in the living room of Hayden and Elle's home, where Abby and Elle were waiting.

"I need Kinsley," Hayden declared.

"Are you sure this is necessary?" Elle asked, already knowing the answer.

"I wish that it wasn't," Hayden said. "I can't face that entire army alone. Amaris will attack and while I'm stuck fighting him, his soldiers will overwhelm me. Then I would have no choice but to level the entire city, with everyone in it, if I wanted to live. Having Kinsley by my side is the best chance we have to make it out of this alive."

"Amaris' army has taken over downtown," Dan added. "It is insane out there."

"Okay," Elle said. "She is asleep in her bedroom. Please protect her."

"Of course I will," Hayden reassured her. "I will be right back with her."

Hayden walked into Kinsley's room and took her from the crib. As he placed her on the carpet and removed her onesie, Kinsley woke. Hayden could hear the television in the living room. It was still showing live footage from Los Angeles, where the chorus of explosions and gunfire raged on. He looked down at Kinsley, noticing that she was silent, as if she was waiting for what was coming.

"Aspiris Dasfiya Ithna 'Ashar," Hayden chanted as he held his hands over Kinsley's body. Bursts of white light exploded all around the bedroom. The particles of light came together and weaved themselves around Kinsley's body. The purple light shining from Hayden's amulet flashed with such intensity that he was forced to shield his eyes. As the light dissipated, Hayden looked down to observe the effects of the spell. Kinsley reached up toward Hayden. He took her hand and they fell into the dreamscape.

Once inside, Kinsley closed her eyes and focused. Hayden could feel that she was accessing a multitude of knowledge from his mind.

"I just needed the history of this reality," she said after opening her eyes again. "Let's go back to the real world now."

Hayden woke, slightly astonished that Kinsley was so adept at manipulating the dreamscape without any help from him whatsoever. Their time inside the construct was so brief, that his body hadn't even fallen to the carpet yet.

"Father," Kinsley said to Hayden. "I'm finally here. It's so good to see you in person."

"You too, Kinsley," Hayden replied.

"Really though?" Kinsley said as she stood up and looked down at her body. "I know our powers manifest at puberty, but you *could have* made me a little older. Kiera gets to be sixteen and what did you age me up to… like twelve?"

"Yeah, twelve," Hayden admitted. "That's how old you looked to be in the dreams… so I just went off of that."

"It's fine… actually, it's ingenious," Kinsley said with a laugh. "Everyone always underestimates a tween girl. I can use that to my advantage. They won't even see me as a threat."

"Well, we can definitely use any advantage that we can scrape up," Hayden said as he walked over to a small table near the door and grabbed a neatly folded pile of clothes. "Here are some old clothes of your mother's. When we were inside the dreamscape, you mentioned just needing the history of *this* reality. What did you mean by that?"

"You saw glimpses of another reality when you were cast adrift in time by Amaris," Kinsley replied as she took the clothes and dressed herself. "I didn't need all the basic knowledge that you taught Kiera in the dreamscape, because I already know all of that from that other reality. I didn't need you to make up a fake childhood for me, because I still remember my childhood from the other timeline. I just needed to know the facts of everything that has happened in this reality since it branched off."

"That all actually happened then?" Hayden asked.

"We have so much that we need to discuss," Kinsley answered. "There is way too much information for us to cover it all right now. We have to go take care of some threat, right?"

"Yes," Hayden admitted. "I tried to avoid needing to age you up. I waited as long as I could… but yes, there is a threat and I need your help."

"So what exactly are we up against?" Kinsley asked as she walked over to the mirror, adjusted her outfit and hastily brushed through her hair. "It's Amaris, right?"

"Yeah, it is Amaris," Hayden replied. "He has an army that he brought with him from the future. He also has your sister, Kiera. She has been under his control and I haven't been able to get through to her so far."

"Okay, we can do this," Kinsley said as she walked up to Hayden and placed her hands on his arms. "After we finish dealing with this, we will talk about everything. There is so much that I need to tell you… and I really just want to spend time with you. I miss you, Dad. I love you."

"I love you too, Kins," Hayden said, the serious look on his face having been replaced with a soft smile. "Everyone is waiting for us in the living room, if you're ready. You might need to give your mom a minute or two for the shock to wear off."

"Okay," Kinsley said as she hugged Hayden for several seconds. "Now, I'm ready."

Hayden opened the bedroom door and stepped

into the hallway to see Elle, Abby, and Dan waiting at the end of the hallway in anticipation. The look on Elle's face when Kinsley stepped out of the bedroom changed from nervousness to astonishment.

"Hi, Mom!" Kinsley exclaimed giddily as she ran down the hallway and hugged Elle. "I love you."

"I love you too," Elle said while immediately bursting into tears.

Hayden walked down the hall and joined everyone else in the living room. After Kinsley made the rounds saying hello to everyone, she walked over to Hayden and stood at his side.

"So, what is our strategy?" Armond asked.

"With two of us, we can fight without having to worry about being blindsided or overrun," Hayden said. "One of us will probably have to take on Amaris while the other keeps the army at bay. At least that's my theory. Anything could happen though. Kiera and Kali haven't been too active in the fight… and Paige is missing in action after I broke through Amaris' control over her mind."

"I don't think we will have a problem," Kinsley said confidently. "As long as we protect each other and work together."

"So, kind of just playing it by ear," Dan joked. "I like

it. Feels like a Hayden move for sure."

"There are two little things that will help," Kinsley said as she turned to Hayden.

"Okay, what's up?" Hayden replied.

"I want to be able to help as best I can," Kinsley said. "When you saw me in your dreams, there was a city."

"I remember the city," Hayden said. "I saw it grow from an empty field, to an enormous metropolis, to ash in a matter of seconds. It was like you were controlling… Oh, it's meant to be you. I had a feeling that it might be."

"That is how I was able to reach out to you," Kinsley affirmed. "You gave it to me in the other timeline also."

"Care to clue us all in?" Dan said. "You two already have a whole superpowered father-daughter secret language going on."

"Bilv'at gave me the ability to name a new Amira al-Dahr," Hayden replied. "It is supposed to be Kinsley."

"You should be cautious about anything from Bilv'at that seems to be a gift," Armond warned.

"I can handle the power," Kinsley said.

"I agree with Kinsley," Hayden said. "Her having those powers may prove very useful."

"Well, there is obviously no point in trying to dissuade you," Armond said. "There never is."

"Agreed," Hayden joked and then faced Kinsley. "Okay, then let's do this."

Hayden placed one hand on Kinsley's chest and with the other he grasped his amulet. "Taeyin masitir Amira al-Dahr."

Kinsley felt an energy swirling to life inside of her as the clock on the wall slowed to a standstill. As quickly as the second hand stopped, time resumed as normal. The windows of the house rattled as a deafening crackle tore across the sky. Kinsley held her palm up and swirls of purple light flowed just above her hand.

"Perfect," Kinsley said.

"Okay, so you said there were two things you needed, right?" Hayden asked. "We took care of the first one. What is the second thing?"

"Since I haven't had any time to train or develop my powers here, I'm a lot weaker than I'm used to." Kinsley replied.

"Obviously, that's no good," Hayden said. "What would help with that though, other than taking time we don't have to develop your powers?"

"I need unfiltered access to large amounts of raw power," Kinsley said as she took Hayden's hands in her own. "I apologize for this in advance, because I know that the type of bond this creates is… profound."

"What are you…" Hayden started to ask before Kinsley interrupted him.

"E'it ad'a layadänte," Kinsley spoke the words of the Forbidden Spell.

The force of the words hit Hayden and an indescribable chill ran through his body. An orb of white light surrounded their joined hands and built into a blinding pulse of energy. The others in the room could see the faint visual of Hayden and Kinsley's auras blurring toward each other until they merged and the two were sent stumbling backward by some invisible force.

Hayden looked down at his left arm. Another marking appeared next to the one he had received when he cast the spell on Elle and himself. Kinsley examined her own arm and confirmed that the same symbol was just above her left elbow.

"Kinsley!" Elle said sternly. "That spell is… how it…"

"I know, Mother," Kinsley replied. "But I need the power and, in the near future, we will need that unparalleled bond. There are things that I must tell him about the past and the future. Things that he cannot just simply hear… he must understand things about me at the core of my soul. I need him to be able to feel my emotions, hear my thoughts, and tap into feelings that cannot be expressed with words."

"Kinsley, still," Elle echoed her previous sentiment.

"It will help us in the fight we are about to face also," Kinsley continued. "We will be able to feel each other's intentions and act accordingly."

"Well, Hayden, that is definitely your daughter," Armond joked. "The unabashed impulsiveness is very reminiscent of you."

"Yeah, yeah," Hayden said. "I get it… taste of my own medicine and whatnot. Duly noted."

"I'm ready when you are," Kinsley said.

"Good luck you two," Abby chimed in.

"Aren't you all coming to watch?" Kinsley asked.

"That's a little dangerous," Elle told her.

"No, it's not. Dad and I will keep you all safe," Kinsley replied. "You can watch from a safe space too."

"Dude, I'm totally down to see the action," Dan said while nudging Abby with his elbow. "From a safe distance this time."

"Sure," Abby reluctantly agreed. "If it's okay with you, Elle."

"Okay, fine. Let's all go," Elle relented. "I should be there anyway for when Kiera needs me."

"Alright, let's go," Kinsley said as she opened a portal

back to Los Angeles.

ɷ ɷ ɷ ɷ ɷ ɷ

Kinsley led the group out of the portal and onto the roof of the condominium building on the corner of Fourth Street and Broadway. From the vantage point, they could see the massive swarm of Amaris' soldiers filling the streets for several blocks. There was fighting between the soldiers and LAPD officers on several fronts. Other groups of Amaris' army were smashing out the windows of buildings and lighting them ablaze.

"I would call this chaos, but I think that's an understatement," Dan said as he looked out over the skyline.

"Don't worry, Dan. We will have this under control soon," Kinsley said before turning to Hayden. "Are you ready?"

"Ready as I'll ever be," Hayden replied.

"Okay, let's do this," Kinsley said with a smile as she walked toward the edge of the roof.

Hayden kissed Elle before joining Kinsley at the roof's edge. The anticipation of the impending battle provided his body with a surge of adrenaline.

"Oh, one last thing. Just in case... Chantiatus," Kinsley said as she turned back to the group and brought up a forcefield around them.

Kinsley and Hayden climbed up on the ledge of the building. The symbol of Air appeared on each of their hands just before they leapt from the roof.

"When we found out that I was pregnant with Kinsley, I teased Hayden that he was seriously outnumbered by us girls," Elle told the group on the roof. "Now I think the joke is kind of on me though. She's like a little female version of him."

"She definitely did inherit Hayden's flair for the dramatic," Abby agreed.

Kinsley and Hayden slowed their descent toward the ground and landed in the middle of Fourth Street. Amaris observed their arrival to the fight from his perch at the edge of California Plaza Park. A group of thirty soldiers immediately swarmed on the father and daughter's location. Hayden readied himself for the attack.

As the soldiers came within arms length, Kinsley knelt down and pressed her palm to the asphalt. A sphere of fire pulsed out twenty feet in all directions, incinerating all of the attackers. The shockwave from the pulse sent the next wave of soldiers flying backward through the air. Hayden faltered for a moment in admiration of Kinsley's talent.

As the shell-shocked soldiers rose back to their feet

and resumed their charge, the symbol of Lightning flashed on the back of Kinsley's right hand. The sky grew dark as ominous clouds appeared and blanketed the sky. A downpour of lightning bolts fell from the clouds and struck dozens of soldiers. Hayden recovered from his brief shock and joined the fray, using both hands to vaporize soldiers with blasts of pure energy.

The sound of thunder rolling through the sky was overpowered as the remainder of Amaris' army turned their attention to Hayden and Kinsley. The roar of thousands of footsteps, accompanied by battle cries, echoed through the streets. The father and daughter duo slowly advanced toward Amaris' location as they downed soldiers. Hayden established a rhythm, alternating between Fire, Lightning, and energy blasts… cutting through his opponents by the dozen. Kinsley continued to show that she wielded great skill in the use of her powers.

With only five hundred feet now between them and Amaris, Kinsley noticed a glint of light reflecting from a broken-out window on the twentieth floor of the skyscraper at the northwest corner of Fourth and Olive. She saw the barrel of a rifle aimed down at their location on the street. Kinsley looked over at Hayden, whose back was turned as he fought off more soldiers.

Before Kinsley had time to act on the threat, the pop of gunfire echoed off the concrete and glass of the surrounding buildings. Kinsley clenched her fists and a bright purple light radiated from her body. The army of soldiers froze in place as time stopped. With only twenty feet between the fired round and Hayden's head, Kinsley reached up and took the bullet in her hand.

Kinsley unclenched her other fist and the time freeze ended. The symbol of Lightning flashed on her hand again. An enormous bolt of electricity streamed from the sky and hit the skyscraper's window. The resultant shower of debris rained down on the city streets over several blocks. Hayden turned to look at her, his eyes wide open in shock.

"Sniper," she said, as she opened her hand and showed Hayden the projectile before tossing it in the gutter. "Almost got you, Dad."

"Thank you," Hayden said. "I suppose you're going to hold that over my head when you want me to buy you a car or something."

"Something like that," Kinsley said as she laughed.

The duo neared Olive Street. The sound of a stampede of boots grew loud behind them. A thousand soldiers rounded the corner behind them at Fourth and Broadway, attempting to flank them with overwhelming force.

Kinsley and Hayden stood in the intersection of Fourth and Olive, awaiting the horde of soldiers. Amaris watched from his vantage point, confident that any action by himself was unnecessary.

As the mass of soldiers crossed Hill Street, a deafening blast roared through the city. An enormous cloud of dust and smoke rose into the air accompanied by a staggering fireball. Once Hayden's field of vision cleared, he saw that portions of Hill Street, Fourth Street, and the surrounding buildings had collapsed into a massive hole in the ground. The impromptu explosion claimed nearly a thousand of Amaris' soldiers in its devastating aftermath.

Hayden looked over at Kinsley who shrugged her shoulders to indicate that she had nothing to do with the blast. The remaining soldiers in the area stopped in place, fearful and confused. Through the dust blanketing the area, Hayden made out the figure of a person walking up Olive Street toward him. As the figure came closer, he was taken aback to see that it was Paige. She walked through groups of soldiers, who were still obeying Amaris' command to regard her as an ally.

"I hope that this makes up for all the wrong I did before," Paige said to Hayden as she arrived in front of him. "For trying to kill you in the movie theater and at Yosemite."

"That wasn't even you," Hayden replied. "You were possessed by the Alva'ci. I don't blame you for that or hold it against you."

"Still, I feel bad for it," Paige said. "Once you freed me from Amaris' control over my mind, I had to do something to help you."

"What exactly did you do?" Kinsley asked.

"Amaris stopped a subway train on the tracks underneath Hill Street and filled it with explosives," Paige said. "He was going to use it as a last act of terror after he won the battle. He was so confident in himself and this army that he only had one soldier down there guarding it. I snuck up and killed the guard and then took the detonator. I was waiting at the Pershing Square station. Once I saw all the soldiers come off of Broadway, I ran down Hill Street and then set off the explosives."

"Well, you definitely took out a huge piece of Amaris' army," Kinsley said. "Well done."

"Are you okay?" Hayden asked Paige.

"Yeah, I'm good," she replied. "A little shook up, a little bruised and bloody… but I'm okay."

"Attack them!" Amaris yelled to his soldiers.

"Chantiatus," Hayden uttered to protect Paige with a forcefield as he saw the soldiers resume their assault.

"There's only about a thousand of them left," Kinsley said to Hayden. "About seven hundred of them are coming at us from the south. Hold off the ones from the north and west. I need a moment to prepare myself."

"You got it," Hayden replied as he went to work eliminating the soldiers that attacked from their sides.

Kinsley closed her eyes and lowered her head in concentration. Hayden noticed that his amulet was glowing brightly as Kinsley drew more and more power from it through her connection with him. Once he had dealt with all of the soldiers in the immediate vicinity, he looked back toward Kinsley. The swarm of bodies were fast approaching and now within twenty feet of her. Kinsley opened her eyes and her hands erupted with pure white light.

Hayden watched in awe as his daughter went on the offensive. She raised her palms toward the remaining members of Amaris' army. A monstrous wall of Fire, infused with Electricity and Shadow tore through the street. Concrete and glass ripped from the buildings lining the road. When the blast finally dissipated after several city blocks of destruction, Hayden looked to see that the remaining soldiers were nothing more than ash in the wind.

"Holy shit," Dan said to the others still watching from the roof of the condominium building on Fourth and

Broadway. "Your daughter is a badass, Elle."

Hayden and Kinsley turned to face Amaris. He stood in the same place, overlooking the street from the edge of California Plaza Park. Kiera and Kali stood at his sides. If Amaris was at all unsure of himself, he did not show any outward display of it. Kinsley, Hayden, and Paige walked up the staircase leading to the overlook.

"Welcome back, Father," Amaris said as they approached.

"Amaris, it is time to finally end this," Hayden replied.

"I agree wholeheartedly," Amaris mocked. "Let's get this out of the way so I can continue my conquest."

"Did you not notice that your army has been destroyed?" Kinsley asked with an obvious attitude.

"A minor setback. I can make more soldiers," Amaris replied as he looked Kinsley up and down. "Well now, aren't you just a darling little cherry blossom?"

Kinsley's demeanor was stoic and still, but Hayden could feel the emotions swirling within her... a flash of rage and a yearning for revenge.

"Did you bring another daughter of yours so that I could take her from you?" Amaris taunted Hayden.

"You're a little too arrogant, don't you think?" Hayden replied.

"Come to me," Amaris told Kinsley, the sound of his voice signifying that he was using the power of Ane'illuminus on her. "Abandon your father and join me."

Kinsley walked toward Amaris as instructed. With each step that she took, the smile on Amaris' face grew wider and more proud. Hayden remained motionless as he focused on Kinsley's thoughts.

"Very good," Amaris said when Kinsley arrived in front of him and he placed his hand on her cheek. "I'll definitely enjoy having you around."

Kinsley mirrored Amaris' actions and placed one of her palms on his cheek. The resultant look in his eyes was menacing and deviant. As Amaris gloated internally in his accomplishment, Kinsley used her other hand to grab his amulet.

"You little…" Amaris exclaimed before using his free hand to hit Kinsley with an energy blast.

Kinsley flew backward through the air, but caught herself mid-flight and descended, unharmed, next to Hayden and Paige.

"I'm not such an easy target you fool," Kinsley said. "I'm not Kiera."

"It doesn't matter," Amaris said. "You don't need to join me. I'll just destroy you both. Oh, and Paige, once you have that baby I'm going to kill you too."

"I'll handle this," Hayden said to Kinsley.

"So eager to lose," Amaris mocked Hayden. "You know, I doubt that Elle and your friends can see much of the action through all the smoke coming from Paige's huge hole in the ground. Why don't we bring them closer, so they can witness your downfall?"

Amaris waved his hand in the direction of the condominium building and portals opened up beneath Elle, Dan, Abby, and Armond. A new set of portals opened behind Hayden and the group fell to the ground.

"Stay back, everyone," Hayden urged as he looked over his shoulder.

"Let's do this!" Amaris yelled as he fired off a blast of energy at Hayden, who easily deflected it into a nearby building.

The two went back and forth, each occasionally landing an attack on the other. Amaris was pleased to show off the increased strength he had attained with the creation of his amulet. Glass and debris rained down into the streets as father and son diverted each other's attacks into the cityscape.

"Attack him!" Amaris commanded Kali and Kiera using the power of Ane'illuminus.

Kiera was the first to obey and fired a continuous

stream of energy toward her father. Kali held out for a few moments before her mind lost control. She joined Kiera in an identical attack. Hayden used his free hand to easily hold their assaults at bay. Amaris took advantage of Hayden's split focus and strengthened his own attacks against him.

Amaris raised his free hand to the sky and a lightning bolt shot down at Elle, striking the forcefield around her. As Hayden looked back at Elle, Amaris' attack hit him. Hayden flew backward and landed between Elle and Abby. He rose to his feet with a frustrated groan.

"I'm okay," Elle assured him.

"This is too easy!" Amaris yelled out to Hayden before turning his attention to Kinsley. "How about you little girl… do you want to have a taste of this power?"

Kinsley refused to answer, but instead closed her eyes and let out an exasperated sigh.

جاليتسور

Chapter Six

Child of Hope

A low hum filled the landscape with no apparent source. Elle turned and looked at Hayden in suspense as the conflict stood at a pause. The air was heavy with tension and anticipation. She was no more comforted by the look in Hayden's eyes as she had been before. Hayden walked back over to Kinsley's side to rejoin the fight.

The humming noise was soon replaced, as a puddle of water near Hayden's feet began to ripple to life. An uneasy feeling grew in the pit of his stomach. The ground shook with light tremors. Elle noticed the fine peach-fuzz blonde hairs on her arms standing at attention as the temperature dropped dramatically.

The sky grew dark, as if nightfall had arrived early. Amaris continued his brazen and arrogant waiting game, simply watching Kinsley as if she were a minor inconvenience. Kiera stood two steps behind him, her concern beginning to grow with the atmospheric changes.

"You want to play with magic?" Kinsley broke the silence, her voice raised over the wind that had begun whipping across the terrace. "Your tricks and your trifling efforts are nothing more than children's games."

The smirk on Amaris' face slowly faded with Kinsley's taunts. His pride would not let her insults abide. As he calculated his response, Kinsley beat him to the first move. Her feet left the ground as she stretched her arms up out at her sides. Kinsley rose into the air and the dark skies began to crackle with energy. Streams of lightning showered the entire city block in a brilliant and deafening chorus of power.

Kinsley swept her arm in front of her and both Kiera and Kali flew in opposite directions away from Amaris. Elle ran over to Kiera to find her unconscious. Kali lay unresponsive near the edge of the terrace. Kinsley followed up with an enormous pulse of energy that sent Amaris tumbling off the side of the terrace to the street, thirty feet below. He immediately rose to his feet and flew back up to the terrace.

"This might be fun," Amaris said as he landed.

"Not for you," Kinsley replied.

Amaris grasped his amulet and used his other hand

to fire off an even larger beam of energy back at Kinsley. She deflected it into a building across the street that crumbled as the immense blast hit it.

After the disappointing result, Amaris decided to switch to melee fighting. He drew the sword from his side and charged Kinsley. The symbol of Light appeared on her hand and a plasma-like blade materialized, that met Amaris' sword with a sharp clang. Kinsley continued to parry his attacks, while landing blows against Amaris using pulses of energy from her free hand. Within two minutes, Kinsley had gained the advantage and Amaris found himself on the defense.

Amaris' anger began to build. He moved his strategy to fighting dirty. As Kinsley came toward him, Amaris opened a portal underneath her. As quickly as she fell into the field, he opened a corresponding portal six feet off the ground behind him. He turned around to see Kinsley falling from the field and he thrust his sword upward at her.

Hayden's amulet flashed in a brilliant purple color as Kinsley stopped time. She descended to the ground and took Amaris' sword from his motionless hand. Kinsley then opened a portal of her own and tossed the sword inside. She walked over near Hayden and Elle, closed her portal, and then released the time freeze.

"What the…" Amaris yelled angrily as his weaponless arm flailed upward. He turned around to face Kinsley again.

"I told you," Kinsley said to him. "You don't know what you're up against, Amaris."

"You think you're so clever and quick," Amaris replied as he grasped his amulet. "I think that it's time I ended this. I have plans to attend to. Prepare yourself to see true power. It will be the last thing you see before the skin melts off that pretty little face of yours and you die an agonizing death."

"You want to know power?" Kinsley replied, thick with attitude and confidence.

Kinsley held her palm to the sky. Every symbol of power cycled in rapid succession on the back of her hand. In the blackness of the sky a dazzling light appeared. A beam of energy shot down. As it neared, the shockwave blasted out any remaining building windows within a twenty block radius. Trees uprooted from the ground and the water in nearby rooftop pools vaporized.

"Oh my God," Elle said, stunned. "I think that she's more powerful than you, Hayden."

"Far more…" Hayden agreed.

Amaris raised his hand in an attempt to deflect or halt the assault, to no avail. He fell to the ground and found himself pinned on his back. Kinsley slowly walked toward him and stopped at his side. She held her arm out at her side and opened a portal. Amaris' sword fell from the portal into her hand. She tilted the blade down at his body, her intention clear.

"Kinsley!" Hayden yelled with no response from her. "Kins!"

She started to thrust the blade down at Amaris when she felt Hayden. For a brief moment, he used the bond between them to commune with her. She stopped her attack and threw the sword back onto the concrete. Hayden gasped and his footing faltered as, for a brief moment, he felt the essence of his daughter's being. He regained his composure and walked to her side, immediately putting his arm around her and drawing her into an embrace. Kinsley momentarily let her guard down and buried her head in Hayden's chest… then returned to a stoic stance at his side. Hayden knelt down next to Amaris.

"You underestimated her because she's young and because she's a girl," Hayden told Amaris. "That was horribly stupid of you."

"What are you going to do with him, Dad?" Kinsley asked.

"There is only one way that he has any chance of being reformed," Hayden replied as he placed his hand on Amaris' amulet. "Aspiris Tahtishna Sifr."

A flash of white light from Hayden's amulet washed out everyone's vision for several seconds. When their sight returned, they no longer saw the young man lying on the concrete. Under the pile of clothes that Amaris had been wearing, the sound of a babbling baby broke the silence on the terrace. Hayden moved the clothing to reveal Amaris, now a six month old infant. He took the second amulet and placed it in his pocket.

Hayden put his hand on the baby's forehead and focused. The infant fell silent as Hayden pulled him into the dreamscape and used his powers to erase all of Amaris' memories and knowledge. A few moments later, they both came back into reality and everything returned to normal.

Kiera's body stirred and she woke up, disoriented and confused. Elle helped her up to her feet and steadied her. Abby walked over to assist and make sure that Kiera was okay.

"Mom?" Kiera said as she hugged Elle. "What happened? Where are we?"

"You're okay sweetheart," Elle told her. Your dad and sister defeated a bad person and we're all safe now."

"I have a sister?" Kiera asked, even more confused.

In the opposite direction, Kali started to wake up. Hayden took the baby and handed him to Dan, who reluctantly took him.

"He's just a baby now, Dan," Hayden said. "Just a normal baby. He's not going to shock you or anything. He's harmless."

"If you say so," Dan joked, moreso to make himself more comfortable than anything.

Hayden and Kinsley approached Kali as she sat up on the concrete. With the deaging of Amaris, all of the effects of his powers had disappeared. Hayden held out his hand and helped Kali to her feet.

"Oh my God, Hayden," she said through sobs. "I am so sorry for everything I've done. I hope that you can find it in your heart to forgive me… to help me. I love you. I want to make things right with you. I want us to be us again."

Hayden could subconsciously feel Elle's glare even though she was behind him and thirty feet away. Kinsley stepped in front of Kali and placed her hand on Kali's chest. Swirls of orange and purple light emanated from Kali's body and flowed into Kinsley.

"She's completely powerless now," Kinsley told Hayden. "I took all the last remnants of anything she had left inside her. She's just a normal girl now. So, do whatever you want with her. Don't be afraid to be merciful, but be wise."

"Thank you, Kins," Hayden replied. "I know that you

can feel the confliction inside me."

"I can," Kinsley agreed. "Whatever you decide, there will be consequences either way. I'm here for you though. You will always have me by your side."

"Please don't kill me, Hayden," Kali cried and she flung her arms around Hayden and pulled him in close. "I just want you to let me love you like I should have all along. Being close to you again feels so right."

Elle's footsteps coming toward them seemed to echo violently throughout the courtyard. Kinsley looked at Hayden with an expression meant to confirm that Elle's demeanor was not happy.

"Hayden… *husband*," Elle said as she arrived at his side. "Your wife and children need you right now. She killed thousands of people. She killed my family."

"Dad…" Kiera said as she walked up. "What would you do if it was me?"

Hayden's head swirled with all of the opposing opinions. He became acutely aware of Kinsley's warning about consequences in this decision. Kali continued to cling tightly to him. He weighed his choices for a moment and then made a verdict.

"Armond, come here please," he called out across the terrace.

As Armond arrived, Hayden pulled himself loose from Kali and looked at her. Elle and Kiera waited to see what Hayden would do.

"No matter what I decide, I know that I am going to disappoint someone," Hayden said. "This is an impossible situation."

Hayden reached out and placed his palm on Kali's forehead. She immediately fell limp into his arms. He picked her motionless body up and handed her to Armond.

"Take her back to your house," Hayden told Armond as he opened a portal next to him. "She is not going to wake up, but she is alive. I will come over later. I implanted a thought in her mind to recognize you as a friend."

"Of course," Armond replied. "I will see you then."

Armond disappeared with Kali through the portal and it snapped shut. Hayden could hear Elle's quickened breathing that conveyed her anger.

"Why?" Elle asked.

"Mom, she wasn't herself when she did all of those things," Kiera said. "Just like I wasn't myself. I could have been forced to do anything, unforgivable things even."

"Kiera, stop please," Elle said. "I would still have my mom and dad if it weren't for her... my brother too. She tried to kill me. She tried to kill you too before you were even born.

The only thing that she actually does want, is your father."

"You don't need to worry about that, Mom," Kinsley said. "He wouldn't betray you."

"Kinsley, I'm sorry but you don't know what you're talking about," Elle replied.

"I know my father," Kinsley said. "I can feel what he feels. You can too, if you'd stop letting your anger get in the way."

"Kins," Hayden said in a hushed tone. "I know you're trying to help. Your mother's feelings are completely understandable and valid given what she's been through. Let her and I work through this together."

"Hayden, just send me home please," Elle said exasperated. "Just open a portal and let me take Kiera back to the house. Kinsley, I assume that *you* want to stay here with your dad."

"I do," Kinsley replied.

Hayden did as asked and opened a portal back to their home in Camarillo. Elle took Kiera's hand and started to walk toward the field.

"We will be there soon," Hayden said. "I love you… both of you."

"Okay, see you," Elle replied.

Just before stepping into the portal, Kiera looked

back over her shoulder with a somber look on her face and mouthed the words, "love you," back to Hayden. The portal snapped shut behind them. Dan and Abby walked up to Hayden.

"That's tough, dude," Dan said as the baby slept in his arms.

"She's just jealous," Kinsley said. "Jealous of what Kali had with you even though that's obviously over… and strangely enough, she's jealous of me also."

"She's hurt, Kins," Hayden replied.

"She's being irrational," Kinsley disagreed. "What does she think you're going to do? Leave her? Leave all of us and run away with someone else? Obviously, your plan doesn't include Kali remaining in love with you. I assume that you're going to wipe Kali's memories or something. Elle needs to calm down and reconcile her feelings."

"Kinsley Rae… do not disrespect your mother," Hayden said sternly. "It may take her some time. Kali being alive is bringing up a lot of old grief, hurt, and anger in her. You cannot be that impatient with her."

"I'm sorry, Dad," Kinsley replied. "I'm impatient because I already know what's going to happen. I'm the Princess of Time now, remember? I can see what is going to happen. I just… it makes me want things to happen more quickly."

"You already know what's going to happen?" Dan asked. "Like you already know what Elle is going to do? What Hayden is going to do?"

"Yeah," Kinsley replied. "I can't see eons into the future or anything… but I know what is going to happen here, with this. To me, it's all unnecessary emotion getting in the way of life. There's not enough time in life to have all of these messy things interfering with being happy."

"Damn…" Abby remarked. "Aristotle over here with the sage wisdom beyond her years."

"Hayden," Paige said as she stood from the bench she had been resting on behind the rest of the group. "Thank you for letting my sister live. I'm sorry for everything that my family has put you through… you and your family. If I can do anything to help you, I will."

"Paige, you are family to me too," Hayden replied. "Just like Dan and Abby are also. You don't need to apologize."

"I just think that if I had never wandered into that stupid cave, none of this would have happened," Paige said. "I feel like it's all my fault. Everyone could have been happy."

"That's not true," Kinsley said. "The Alva'ci would have still come. The world would actually be in worse shape."

"Wait a second," Dan interrupted. "Are you saying

that you know like alternate realities or something?"

"Yeah," Kinsley replied. "Technically, there is only one stream of reality, of time… but it can branch off if there is a significant change made. I know what would have happened in the alternate timeline, because I lived it."

"So, you were in the alternate timeline?" Dan asked.

"Yes, I was in the alternate timeline," Kinsley confirmed. "I was still born. So was Kiera. My mother and father still ended up together. That is a fact that is constant, no matter the timeline. They would always find each other, always fall in love, always have me. There are just some things that are destined to be and cannot be changed."

"That's kind of sweet and romantic," Abby said. "In a crazy sci-fi kind of way."

"So Paige," Hayden said, redirecting the conversation back to her. "You're pregnant?"

"I am pregnant," Paige concurred. "Almost seven weeks. Amaris wanted an heir for his plans of world domination. He… impregnated me."

"I'm sorry that you had to go through that," Hayden said. "That you have to deal with that now. What do you want to do?"

"I think that I'm going to have the baby," Paige admitted. "I've always liked babies, always wanted one someday. I mean, I might need some therapy to go along with it though."

"We're always here to help you," Abby insisted. "It's great to have you back."

"I guess now the owners of Eduardo Quesada's can take your memorial picture down," Dan said.

"They put up a picture?" Paige asked.

"Yeah right in the main lobby," Dan replied. "I guess you were one of their favorite customers."

"They're going to freak out if I walk back in there for dinner," Paige joked.

"We should get to it, Dad," Kinsley interrupted. "You and I have a lot to do and even more to discuss."

"Yes, daughter," Hayden said in a jokingly compliant tone.

"So, what are we going to do with…" Dan asked as he nodded his head down at the baby in his arms.

"Can you and Abby hang on to the baby for a while?" Hayden asked. "Until I sort things out a little bit."

"Yes!" Abby replied excitedly. "Maybe it'll be good practice for you, Dan."

"Practice?" Dan stuttered as his eyes widened.

"I'm not pregnant," Abby replied. "I'm just saying… maybe one day."

"Oh, well practice sounds good," Dan said. "Do you want to stay with us for now, Paige?"

"Yeah, if that's okay with you?" Paige asked.

"Of course it is," Abby replied.

Hayden opened a portal back to Abby's apartment and the rest of the group departed through it, leaving only him and Kinsley remaining on the terrace. Together, they looked out over the destruction that blanketed downtown.

"Time to go take care of Kali now?" Kinsley asked.

"Yeah," Hayden replied with a long sigh. He opened a portal and they walked through.

℘ ℘ ℘ ℘ ℘ ℘

Kinsley and Hayden stepped out into Armond's home, where he was waiting for them in the living room.

"She is in one of the guest rooms," Armond advised Hayden.

Upon entering the bedroom, they found Kali placed on the bed and still unconscious. Hayden placed his hand on her arm and entered the dreamscape. The scene inside was peaceful and serene. Kali stood in front of him and Kinsley was at his side.

"How do you feel Kali?" Hayden asked.

"I feel good," she replied. "I feel normal again. There's just all of that horrible stuff that happened. I know that I'm responsible for all of it."

"You weren't exactly yourself," Hayden said. "That blast of power from the Alva'ci corrupted your mind. I don't know if you can really be blamed for all that happened."

"Maybe so, but I'm still responsible," Kali replied. "People will still look to me to pay for all the crimes and atrocities that occurred."

"Well, no one knows that you're alive," Hayden said. "Except for a very small group of people."

"All that I really want is for things to go back to normal," Kali said. "To be the way that they used to be. You and I had finally figured things out and we were together… we were happy. When the Alva'ci kidnapped me, the last thing that I thought of before it put me under, was you. No other person or thing was in my mind… just you."

"What was normal then… it's not *normal* now," Hayden said.

"That's right," Kali replied. "You're with someone else now. Amaris said that you married her and had kids with her."

"Yeah," Hayden said. "This is one of my daughters, Kinsley. Things can't go back to how they were before."

"I don't know if I can live with that," Kali said.

"Well, that's why I'm here," Hayden told her. "To make it so that you can go on and have a clean slate."

"You're going to erase yourself from my memory?" Kali asked sadly.

"Not completely," Hayden said. "Before you and I were romantically involved, we were friends. I'm going to erase the parts where we were more than friends. I'm also going to take all the traumatic memories from the things that have happened."

"I suppose it's better to still have you as a friend, than as nothing at all," Kali concluded.

"Just understand, I'm not doing this to hurt you or punish you," Hayden said as he placed his hand on the side of Kali's head. "It might not seem like it now, but this is for you. I did love you, Kali… very much. I saw a future together. It just didn't happen. We were pieces of each other's stories, not the entire thing… and that's okay. Now, you'll be able to continue your story."

A tear rolled down Kali's cheek as she looked into Hayden's eyes. He focused and began to pull the memories from Kali's mind. Several minutes passed with Hayden using his memory as a guide to delicately alter Kali's. Kinsley walked up to her father's side and took his hand to offer her support.

"I think that's it," Hayden said to Kinsley after another few minutes of concentration. "I believe that I got everything."

"Okay, then we should probably get back home," Kinsley said.

"Yeah, you're right," Hayden replied as he brought them out of the dreamscape.

The duo walked back down the hallway into Armond's living room, where Hayden explained what he had done with her memories.

"I will look after her for now," Armond said. "I have all of these spare bedrooms, so a roommate will be a welcome change. It will allow me to keep an eye on things also."

"Thank you," Hayden said. "Let me know when you think she is ready and we will bring the baby for her to raise. She is still unconscious, but should wake up in about ten minutes."

"Okay," Armond replied. "You should probably get back home. It sounded like you had more damage control to attend to there. Good luck."

Hayden nodded and opened a portal back to Camarillo. After Kinsley and her father stepped inside, Armond walked down to the bedroom to check on Kali.

ఌ ఌ ఌ ఌ ఌ ఌ

"Mom is in the bedroom," Kiera said as Hayden and Kinsley appeared in the living room. "I think she's asleep now because I haven't heard her crying in about fifteen minutes."

"Okay, thank you," Hayden said after a deep protracted sigh.

"Are you guys going to be alright?" Kiera asked.

"Yeah, Kay, we will be fine," Hayden said. "Everything is just confusing and raw right now. Your mom just needs some time to process everything."

"I hope so," Kiera said. "I just got back to you guys. You better not break up. She's pretty upset and sad… and really angry."

"You let me worry about that," Hayden replied. "Right now, I need you to go into the dreamscape with me. I need to find the moment in time that Amaris was able to manipulate you."

Kiera nodded her head and Hayden sat next to her on the couch. They entered into a blank canvas within the dreamscape and Hayden placed his hand on her forehead.

"He was plotting all along," Hayden said as he found the moment in time he was searching for. He focused in and made sure that there were no residual effects.

"So, what happened?" Kiera asked as she opened her eyes again, back in the living room. "When was it?"

"When he first introduced himself to your mother and I. He came over to the apartment. He touched your cheek when you were a baby. That's when he pushed a thought into your mind. I can't believe that I didn't sense that. He was practically using your own powers against you to make you more susceptible to his influence."

"It's gone now, though?" Kiera asked.

"Yes, it's gone," Hayden confirmed. "Everything looks normal. If you ever want to talk about anything that happened during that time, I am here for you. You can talk to me about anything."

"Okay," Kiera replied. "Right now I just need some rest. I'm so tired and drained."

"Alright, go ahead and get some sleep," Hayden said.

"Hey Kins," Kiera added through a yawn. "You can sleep in my room if you want to. I don't think you'll fit in the crib that is still in your room."

"Thanks, I'll be in there in a minute," Kinsley replied.

"I'll have to switch that crib out for a bed this week," Hayden said, adding the task of his mental to-do list.

"It's weird to think that just a few hours ago, I was in this house as a baby," Kinsley said to Hayden as Kiera disappeared into her bedroom. "Now I'm back here and definitely not a baby."

"Yeah, it's an adjustment, for sure," Hayden agreed.

"We have a lot to talk about," Kinsley said.

"I know, Kins," Hayden replied. "It's late though and I need to check on your mother. Can we postpone it until tomorrow?"

"Of course," Kinsley said. "I'm actually really exhausted. Goodnight, I love you."

"Love you too, Kins," Hayden replied and then walked toward his bedroom.

Hayden entered the room and saw that Elle was already asleep. He contemplated waking her up to talk, but decided against it. Instead, he crawled into bed and stared at the ceiling… contemplating if there was possibly a combination of words that he could say to make everything right again. He fell asleep before coming up with a suitable answer.

೪ ೪ ೪ ೪ ೪ ೪

The Next Morning

Kiera set her plate of freshly-toasted frozen waffles down on the dining room table and sat down next to Kinsley. The younger sister was already in the process of devouring her plateful of waffles.

"How long do you think they're going to do this?" Kiera asked Kinsley, referencing the argument that Hayden and Elle had been having for the past hour.

"A while, I fear," Kinsley replied in between bites.

"I think I might be to blame," Kiera said. "I told Dad that I thought he should forgive Kali."

"It's not your fault," Kinsley disagreed. "Mom is experiencing some complex emotions. It's not really that surprising given all of the crazy events of the past few years. There are things from her past that have had a lingering effect on her self-confidence, even now. Even though she *knows* that Dad wouldn't ever leave her for someone else... everything that's going on with Kali being alive is just stirring those emotions up. I'm sure that she's also experiencing a relapse of grief from losing her parents and brother to a disaster that Kali caused."

"Wow," Kiera stuttered. "How do you know all of that?"

"I just do," Kinsley replied, not wanting to explain it.

In their bedroom, Elle and Hayden continued the tense conversation. Hayden attempted to mostly listen to what Elle was vocalizing, speaking only to answer her questions or accusations.

"She's always going to want you back," Elle said, in reference to Kali. "You dated her, you loved her. Can you actually say that you would never consider getting back with her?"

"I would never consider it," Hayden answered confidently. "As far as what she wants, I erased all of the memories in her head that even remotely pointed at romance between us. To her, we are nothing more than friends that knew each other as children."

"Yeah, well what if that doesn't work?" Elle asked insistently. "What if she makes you fall for her again? I mean, theoretically, you could just erase my memory of you and then go be with her. I wouldn't ever know the difference."

"Elle, I would never alter anything in your mind," Hayden said sternly. "I would never fall for her again, even if she tried to make me. You are my wife. You are the only one I love."

"Hayden, I know how things work," Elle replied. "Sure, you married me… but that doesn't mean that you won't get tired of being with me. Do you remember that night, years ago… when I was at a middle school dance and I called you crying from the school bathroom?"

"Yes, I remember," Hayden confirmed. "I came and picked you up. We spent the rest of the night together at the coffee shop."

"Yeah, and I was crying because the boy that asked me to the dance ran off with some other girl," Elle said. "He literally left me alone on the dance floor. That's not the only time something like that happened to me. I had like two boyfriends after that. Both of them left me for some other girl. It didn't matter how much I liked them. It didn't matter how good, or sweet, or smart, or pretty I was… they still ditched me when some other girl came along that they liked more. So, you know what I've learned?"

"I think so," Hayden replied.

"I learned that most guys are full of crap," Elle continued. "I also learned that in the end, I always get left. Every time, it's like I'm standing there in the middle of the dance floor in the junior high gymnasium, with everyone else looking at me… pointing, laughing, thanking God that they weren't me."

"Elle…" Hayden tried to interject.

"You were like my knight in shining armor that night," Elle said. "You rescued me from all of that embarrassment… and then you turned the whole night around. The dancing, the talking, the coffee shop. You made me feel so special that night. I know that we weren't even thinking about each other romantically back then… but the way you made me feel was incredible. I felt wanted, beautiful, recognized, and worthy. It felt like I was the only girl in the universe to you. It is one of my most cherished memories. I went to sleep that night with such hope inside me. Right now, though, I feel this huge pit in my stomach. It's like I'm waiting for the other shoe to drop. Like any minute, you're going to abandon me."

"I remember that night," Hayden replied. "I love that memory too. It was a special night… and looking back on it now, it was a milestone, even if we were oblivious to it then. It was a step along the path that led us to being together. That is a path that I will never stray from or walk backwards on. I know that I can sit here and say all of these words to you, but unless you let me in… unless you let me be your safe harbor, the words aren't going to do anything to ease your mind."

"That is true," Elle said. "The words… I want to believe them all. Maybe I even know in my heart that I should believe them… but my guard is up. My past experiences with relationships are haunting me, because they tell me that this only ends in one way. I need to see that this is different from everything else I experienced as a girl. Everything that is ingrained in my psyche."

"Okay," Hayden said. "Then you will see it. Right now, we take a momentary truce from arguing about it. The words are just going back and forth with no real effect. We will work this out."

"I hope so, because I've never loved anyone like I love you," Elle replied.

"Elle, babe," Hayden added. "I didn't even know what love actually was… until I loved you."

"Dan and Abby are here!" Kinsley's voice shouted from the other side of the bedroom door.

"Oh, of course, Kinsley is here to get you," Elle said as she rolled her eyes.

"I don't even want to know what you mean by that," Hayden replied.

"What I mean, is that girl has an unusual fixation with you," Elle said.

"That girl?" Hayden replied. "You mean our daughter?"

"Go ahead. I'll be out in one minute," Elle said to Hayden. "I just need to rinse my face off."

Hayden took Elle's hands and squeezed them, then opened the door and followed Kinsley down the hallway.

"How'd it go?" Kinsley asked.

"Kins, not now, please," Hayden replied.

"I told you that she's jealous of me," Kinsley said. "I heard what she said about me through the door."

"That's not helping," Hayden told her.

"Just saying," Kinsley muttered under her breath,

prompting Hayden to look sideways at her.

"Hey, dude," Dan said when Hayden arrived in the living room with Kinsley. "Armond said that all is good there and we can bring the baby over this morning. How are things on the home front?"

"Not ideal," Kinsley butted in.

"It will be okay," Hayden said. "Just a little rough of a morning. Maybe Elle seeing that nothing exists between me and Kali, in person, will help."

"Hopefully," Abby chimed in. "By the way, this baby is pretty cool. He slept all night and is pretty calm when he's awake."

"Getting baby fever?" Hayden joked.

"Maybe," Abby said as she blushed.

"Okay, so back to business," Hayden said. "When we get over to Armond's, please remember that Kali's memory has been altered. I had to erase some things from her past. So she will be confused if you bring certain things up. Specifically, everything about her involvement with the Alva'ci and then anything about her and I having any romantic involvement. So, she does remember the Alva'ci attack, but not that she was kidnapped or anything after that point. Also, she remembers me as a friend from childhood, but not that we ever dated or that she ever had any interest in me. As far as baby Amaris is concerned, she doesn't know who the father is."

"Oh, wow," Abby said. "Honestly, that's kind of messed up… don't you think? Making her forget all those parts of her life. I know that if you did that to me, I would be pissed off."

"Uhh, yeah," Hayden said after an awkward silence where he and Dan made quick eye contact. "It was necessary in order for Kali to lead a normal life without all the trauma from her past. It was needed for all of us to continue on."

"Okay, well I'll go along," Abby said reluctantly.

"Good morning," Elle said to everyone as she emerged from the bedroom.

"Morning, Elle," Abby replied. "How are you today?"

"Been better, but I'll survive," Elle said.

"Well, let's all get over to Armond's house," Hayden interjected after a few moments of silence between the group.

ц ц ц ц ц ц

The group arrived at Armond's home where he and Kali were waiting for them in the living room. Kali was in high spirits and everything appeared to be normal.

"Here's your baby, Kali," Dan said as he handed

Amaris to her. "He was great. If you ever need an overnight babysitter again, I'm sure Abby won't mind us watching him."

"Thank you guys," Kali said. "I appreciate it so much."

"Hi there, I'm Kinsley… I am Hayden's daughter," she said as she held out her hand for Kali to shake.

"Hayden's daughter? Wow, you are so beautiful. Well it's very nice to meet you," Kali replied. "I'm Kali. I've known your father since we were little kids.

"She definitely takes after her mother in the looks department," Hayden said to Kali before pointing out the rest of the family. "This is my eldest daughter Kiera. Do you remember my wife, Elle?"

"Vaguely, I'm sorry," Kali said as she turned to Elle and smiled. "You had visited her and her family back when you were still going to Cal State Fullerton, right? You've known her since you were younger also?"

"Yeah," Hayden replied. "We got married last year."

"Oh, congratulations," Kali said. "It feels like forever since we've hung out. We should all go get dinner or something together and catch up."

"We're always down for dinner," Dan said.

"Hayden, can I speak with you briefly outside?" Armond asked.

Hayden and Dan followed Armond out onto the back

porch to discuss his observations of Kali that morning. Kiera and Kinsley sat on the couch, distracting themselves with a tablet they had brought. Elle excused herself to the restroom while Abby and Kali continued speaking with each other.

"So yeah, Paige will be back tonight from your parent's house," Abby said to Kali. "Maybe we can all go out then."

"That would be amazing. I feel like I haven't been out in forever," Kali replied, before changing to a more hushed tone. "Is Hayden going to go? Like, I know he's married and all… but I should have made him more than just my friend when I was younger. He's a ten out of ten."

"Oh, hey Elle," Abby said in a raised voice as she saw Elle walking up behind Kali's back as she returned from the restroom… obviously within earshot to hear what Kali had just said.

Elle walked directly to the sliding glass door leading to the back porch and stuck her head out. "Hayden, the girls and I will be waiting in the car. Please make this quick."

Hayden knew something was amiss from the look on Elle's face and her immediate departure through the front door with Kiera and Kinsley. Abby rushed out to the back patio as soon as Elle was gone.

"Oh my God," Abby said, panicked and in a whispered voice. "Kali said something about you. Elle had gone to the bathroom, but was walking back out when Kali said it. She definitely heard. Seems like even without her memories, Kali still has a thing for you Hayden."

"I'm so sorry," Kali said apologetically as Hayden entered the living room. "I didn't mean to get you in trouble."

"I've got to go," Hayden replied and walked out the front door.

"Wow," Kali said as she turned back to Abby. "My bad. I didn't know Elle was so touchy. I mean, if she's going to react like that, then maybe I will get my chance with Hayden after all."

مأمون

Chapter Seven

In Another Life

The car ride back to Camarillo was damningly silent. Hayden went over the scene at Armond's house in his head multiple times, trying to figure out what broke down in Kali's memory erasure. As the family pulled into the driveway, everyone quietly shuffled out of the car and into the home.

"Looks like whatever you did, didn't work," Elle said right after they got inside.

"I see that," Hayden replied. "I am sure it's just her talking… reflecting on the past that she knows. I don't think it's serious. It can easily be rebuffed."

"I think it's more like being into you is part of who she is," Elle disagreed. "I think that no matter what you do, it's always going to be like this… and she isn't going to stop until she gets you."

"I will take care of it," Hayden said. "I will fix it."

"I want some time alone," Elle declared.

"Time alone?" Hayden asked, confused.

"Yeah, I want to think," Elle continued. "Without you here. Just some time alone to gather my thoughts and feelings. I think that you should go stay at the apartment in Fullerton for now."

"Separate?" Hayden asked. "You mean temporarily, right?"

"Hopefully," Elle replied. "Just let me have some time alone. If you're here, then it's just going to make me think about all this even more."

"Okay," Hayden said defeated.

"I'll call you in a day or two," Elle said. "The girls can stay here with me."

Kinsley walked closer to Hayden and Elle as if she wanted to butt in to the conversation.

"Oh, wait, what am I thinking," Elle said, with sarcasm now masking her voice, as she saw Kinsley walk up to them. "Let me guess... Kinsley, you want to go with your father?"

"Yeah," Kinsley replied.

"Of course you do," Elle said as she rolled her eyes.

"Whatever, go."

Kiera walked over and hugged Elle as Hayden and Kinsley walked out the front door to leave for Fullerton.

ɕ͡ɜ ɕ͡ɜ ɕ͡ɜ ɕ͡ɜ ɕ͡ɜ ɕ͡ɜ

Kinsley and Hayden pulled into the driveway of the Fullerton apartment. Hayden immediately slumped down on the couch once they were inside. Kinsley paced about the living room as if she were deep in thought.

"Well, at least now we can talk uninterrupted," Kinsley said finally.

"Way to look on the bright side, Kins," Hayden replied sarcastically. "Nevermind that your mother and I are sleeping in different houses tonight."

"You know, you could have just taken the easy way out and killed Kali," Kinsley said. "Then you wouldn't be dealing with all of this. Instead, all of your friends would slowly grow to resent you and hate you for basically murdering her. Like it or not, this is the path you need to take."

"So I was destined to be screwed either way," Hayden said. "That's awesome."

"Dad, just persevere," Kinsley told him. "This will get resolved. Elle just needs some time, just like she said. All you need to do is make it clear, to both Kali and Elle, that you have no interest in Kali. Just make that known, over and over. Trust me."

"You know what's going to happen, don't you?" Hayden asked, choosing not to acknowledge that Kinsley was calling her mother by her first name again.

"I do," Kinsley confirmed. "I can see the future… in a limited sense."

"Why only in a limited sense?" Hayden asked. "Bilv'at was apparently able to see thousands of years into the future."

"I'm not entirely sure," Kinsley admitted. "What is more important right now though, is the past."

"Okay, what about the past?" Hayden asked.

"I have a lot of things to tell you," Kinsley said. "A lot of things to show you… and I have a confession to make."

"Confession?" Hayden prodded.

"Yeah, I changed things," Kinsley said. "When Amaris threw you into those time flashes, you saw a bunch of different fragments of time. A few of the flashes were things that you remember happening. Those were the ones where you could interact with what was happening. The other ones, where you couldn't interact and it seemed like an alternate history… those things actually happened also. They just happened in the timeline at a point after I changed it."

"They happened, but I don't remember them," Hayden said. "I remember the history that actually happened to me. So, what you're saying is that the alternate timeline *was* the real history until you changed something and the timeline kind of branched off into a new reality… this reality."

"Exactly," Kinsley agreed.

"Wait, so what did you change?" Hayden asked, intrigued. "Why did you change things… like seriously enough to alter history?"

"That's what I need to show you," Kinsley said, her voice now softer than Hayden had ever heard it before.

"Okay, so how do we do this?" Hayden asked.

"I'm going to use the same spell that Amaris used to dislodge you from time," Kinsley replied. "The only difference is that I actually know what I'm doing. I can control it."

"Okay, let's do this," Hayden said.

"Dad, there was a reason I changed things," Kinsley said. "When I made the changes and altered the timeline, there were side effects. Unintended casualties. For example, you saw in the alternate timeline that Paige never died at the hands of the Alva'ci in Yosemite. When history changed because of me, she ended up dying in that cave. She's back now, obviously, but she still died because of me… and that's just one example."

"You must have had a good reason," Hayden replied.

"To me, it was the only choice that I had," Kinsley said. "I can't just tell you about it, with words. I need to take you there. I need you to *understand* it. I didn't cast the Forbidden Spell on us just because I needed access to more power. That was one reason, but honestly I could have gotten by without access to your power. The actual reason was that I needed to have the deep bond with you that comes along with the spell… in order for you to truly understand."

"Okay," Hayden said, but was otherwise speechless.

"I'm warning you," Kinsley continued. "With the bond, you are going to feel all of my raw emotions and thoughts. You are going to experience my history as though you were me. You will know the depths of my mind, body, and soul more thoroughly and intimately than anyone ever has or ever will. I'm telling you this to try and prepare you, but honestly no amount of preparation will come close to being enough."

"You're my daughter," Hayden said. "Whatever you need, I will always be there for you. Whatever you need me to experience now, I am here for you."

"I know, thank you. Okay, let's go… I'm sorry." Kinsley said in rapid succession before taking a deep breath and focusing on her powers. "Chronish'balseivius Parov."

ɔ ɔ ɔ ɔ ɔ ɔ

March 28, 2040 - Alternate Timeline
Montana Settlement

Kinsley and Hayden appeared in a location that Hayden had seen before during his flashes through time. It was the settlement in Montana where they had started their own little post-apocalypse town. As Hayden looked around, he noticed that the settlement had grown even larger. He determined that more time must have passed since the time flash he last saw it in. He noticed that everything in the town was perfectly still and there were no sounds to be heard.

"When is this?" Hayden asked Kinsley.

"We are in the year 2040," she replied. "This is March twenty-eighth, the day after my eleventh birthday. I was born on a different day in the alternate timeline, obviously. I have time frozen in place right now so you can take a moment to orient yourself."

"Wow, the settlement lasted all the way until 2040?" Hayden asked. "This place is a lot bigger than when I saw it."

"Yeah, a lot of people took refuge here," Kinsley

replied. "It became a thriving town under the guidance of you and Elle. There were a lot of good, happy people here."

Hayden looked around for a few more moments. Kinsley unfroze time for about sixty seconds before stopping it once again.

"That's Amaris," Hayden said as he observed the teenage boy walking near one of the cabins. "I saw a flash before where he had been born in Florida and Kali told some of her followers to bring him here."

"They did as she commanded," Kinsley said. "They waited until he was four years old and then departed from Florida. It took them a while to get here because they were walking the entire way. They also had to avoid contaminated cities and groups of raiders. They dropped Amaris in front of the town gates when he was ten years old. Kali's followers instructed him to hide any powers that he developed after puberty. At this point in time, he is seventeen."

Kinsley released the time freeze. Hayden watched as Amaris walked down the road and disappeared from view. The front door opened on the cabin that Kinsley and Hayden were standing in front of. Kiera walked outside and waited for her friend to arrive before leaving with her.

A few minutes later, Dan walked up and knocked on the front door of the cabin. He was accompanied by Abby,

Paige, and several other men and women. The door opened and the group was greeted by the alternate timeline version of Hayden and Elle.

"Are you two ready for this hunting trip?" Dan asked loudly.

"Yep, got everything right here," Hayden replied as he grabbed his backpack and Elle's duffel bag.

The entire group walked down the road to a nearby stable, where they switched their method of travel from foot to horseback. A couple minutes later, they were gone from view.

"Okay, let's fast forward here a little," Kinsley said as she altered the speed of time. "There we go. Nine o' clock that night."

Hayden's vision took a moment to unblur from the time alteration. Once he was able to focus back in, he saw that the town was mostly quiet. Everything seemed peaceful. Kinsley began walking toward the cabin and Hayden followed her. They walked along the side of the house and reached the backyard. A figure stood at the rear door, barely visible in the shadows.

Kinsley waved her hand in front of her. She and Hayden flashed to the interior of the cabin. On the dining room wall a banner with the words "Happy Birthday" still hung prominently from the day before. The sound of someone fidgeting with the doorknob on the rear door was barely audible. Kinsley led Hayden down the hallway and they approached the only door that had light peeking out from underneath it.

As they entered the room, Hayden saw the alternate version of Kinsley. She was lying on her stomach on the bed, listening to music from an old cassette player and writing in a journal. The sudden flood of thoughts and emotions hit Hayden like a tidal wave. Just as he had been warned, he could feel everything that alternate Kinsley felt. Every thought that went through her mind felt to Hayden as if he were thinking it himself also. The itch on her left calf… itched on Hayden's as well. He felt the sensation of it being scratched when Kinsley reached down and dragged her fingernails along her leg. Hayden could feel her breathing, her heartbeat… the happiness and contentment she felt as she sung the lyrics to the song that quietly played in the background. The thoughts that became words on the journal's paper in front of her flickered in his mind just before she wrote them down. He felt the surge of panic and the knot in her stomach as the sound of the cabin's back door opening echoed through the home.

Time froze again. Kinsley turned to her father and

looked at him. Her eyes were serious and sad.

"You can feel her, right?" Kinsley asked.

"Yes, I can feel every emotion. I can feel her breathing. Every thought in her head is in mine also," Hayden answered. "It's extraordinary. It's baffling. It's like nothing else I've ever experienced."

"Yeah, which is why I'm really sorry for this," Kinsley said as she unfroze time again. "I won't interrupt time again. Remember everything in this room."

Alternate Kinsley sat up on her bed and peered over at the door while listening for any more sounds in the house. Hayden could feel the fear inside her and the thoughts that she was using to try and convince herself that everything was okay. The shock was palpable when the bedroom door flung open.

Hayden turned to see the figure that had been at the cabin's rear door. It was Amaris. Hayden's breathing deepened as alternate Kinsley's did.

"What are you doing here, Amaris?" she asked.

"Hey there, cherry blossom," Amaris replied. "I'm just here to take action while I still can. I figure that, at most, I only have a few months left before you get your powers."

"What do you mean by that?"

"I think you're cute," Amaris revealed. "I want you."

"I'm not interested," she replied coldly.

"I know," Amaris said as he walked toward her. "Hence, the need for me to take matters into my own hands."

Hayden felt her heartbeat speed up immensely. Fear coursed through his veins in response to her flight or fight instinct. He felt the pain in his bicep as Amaris grabbed alternate Kinsley's upper arm and squeezed it. Her emotions and thoughts blurred and jumbled as she tried to wrest her way from his grip. Hayden could feel his own body growing hotter as he watched alternate Kinsley panic and struggle to free herself.

Pain shot through his other arm as Amaris took hold with his free hand and pushed alternate Kinsley back onto the bed. A fleeting sense of hope flashed through his head when she landed a kick against his thigh and wrestled one arm free. The hope was quickly dashed though.

"Don't be stupid," Amaris said as he activated powers that no one in the town knew he possessed. A small flame appeared in his palm. Hayden could feel the heat on his cheek as Amaris moved it closer to alternate Kinsley's face. "I can make this incredibly painful, but I'd rather not have to fight and kill everyone in this town as a result. I kind of like this little settlement."

Hayden felt the wetness on his cheeks and tasted the

slight tingle of salt on his lips as tears began to roll down alternate Kinsley's face. For a moment there were no thoughts… just a feeling akin to being suffocated. Amaris put the flame out and moved his hand to the waistband of her pajama shorts. Hayden felt a numbness overtaking his mind and a concerted effort to not think as he saw Amaris pull the shorts off.

"Kins! Stop time!" Hayden yelled. She didn't answer him with anything other than a silent shake of her head in the negative.

Hayden's attention jolted back as he felt a harsh scratch in his vocal cords as alternate Kinsley screamed out for help. The cascade of feelings that tore into his mind, body, and soul in the next few minutes as Amaris assaulted alternate Kinsley were overwhelming and devastating. The physical and mental pain seared through every part of his body as they happened in sync with her. He felt every horrifying sensation, every desperate thought, every parching gasp for air through an inflamed throat.

A moment of fearful relief came when Amaris stood up and adjusted his clothing. He walked toward the bedroom door before turning around.

"Remember… you say a word about this and everyone you know dies," he said as he briefly relit the flame in his palm. Then he was gone.

Kinsley stopped time and turned to Hayden. He had no words to speak, but his eyes said everything. She waved her hand in front of her again and they flashed out of the cabin and into an office building.

"We can talk about that when we get back home," Kinsley said. "For now, just watch... I need to show you what exactly I changed."

A uniformed man that Hayden had never seen before walked through the rows of office cubicles and entered a corner office. They followed him inside and found the man silently standing in front of alternate Kinsley, who was now thirteen years old. Hayden looked over at the desk to see a name placard that read, "Lt. Gen. Pierce."

"What is going on?" Hayden asked his daughter.

"Just watch," she replied.

Alternate Kinsley touched the man's forehead and he immediately turned around. He walked over to the large windows that lined the outer edges of the office and calmly opened one. It was then that Hayden noticed they were on the twentieth floor of the building. The man silently and placidly let his body fall forward through the open window. The next sound that Hayden heard was the man's body hitting the concrete below. Alternate Kinsley opened a portal and left.

"You did that with Ane'illuminus. Why?" Hayden asked Kinsley.

"Just keep watching," she said as she flashed them to another moment in time.

Hayden observed as alternate Kinsley repeated the silent assassinations a dozen more times with different men and women. All of them appeared to be high level military or intelligence personnel from the United States, China, and Russia.

"This is it," Kinsley finally spoke as they flashed into the final assassination scene and Hayden watched another person leap to their death. "This is the moment of divergence in the timelines."

"I felt it," Hayden replied. "It almost felt like when you wake up from a dream suddenly… like a ripple in time."

Father and daughter then flashed back to the living room of the Fullerton apartment. All of the memories and feelings that Hayden had experienced in the Montana cabin came rushing back to him. Kinsley followed as Hayden ran to the bathroom and vomited in the toilet.

"How are you?" Kinsley asked after Hayden stopped retching and stood back up.

"Kins," Hayden said quietly. "I'm so sorry."

Hayden looked in the bathroom mirror and saw bruises covering his upper arms, corresponding with the places where Amaris had held alternate Kinsley down.

"I hurt all over," Hayden said to her as he pulled up his shirt to reveal more bruises. He ran his hand along his thighs and could tell that they were also severely bruised. "There's pain in my throat like I was screaming. My arms, legs, chest, stomach, everywhere. I can still feel all of the emotions and thoughts. I feel like it happened to me."

"I'm sorry," Kinsley said. "You understand now… why I changed the timeline."

"I do," he replied. "Kins, I'm here for you. For whatever you need."

"I know you are," she said. "I'll explain the flashes after the Montana cabin. All of those people that leapt to their deaths were the people that would eventually be directly responsible for leading the world into the nuclear war that destroyed everything in the alternate timeline. Those flashes all took place in early 2022. Everything in history that happened before that point is all one timeline. When that last person jumped out the window, the possibility of nuclear war ended. That catalyst was enough to branch the timeline off into what *you* know as the *real* one. The alternate, or original, timeline ceased to exist past that point. Well, it still exists in

some sort of extra-dimensional space as a discarded reality…
that's why you and I can still view it, but it has no bearing on
the reality that is now."

"You like crossed over though… between the alternate
and the real timelines," Hayden said. "How did you do that?"

"I'm the Princess of Time," she replied. "After Amaris
assaulted alternate me, I was not okay. Actually, you know
exactly how I felt. I started puberty six months after that
happened and my powers appeared. Alternate Kali came
back and tried to kill alternate Hayden again. Long story
short, she lost and alternate you ended up giving alternate me
the powers of Amira al-Dahr. I spent all the time that I wasn't
wallowing in depression researching the exact moments in
time I would need to change to prevent the history that I knew
as real. Shortly after I turned thirteen, I went back in time to
2022 and carried out my plan. As the timeline was branching
and my reality was tearing away, I used one of the powers of
the Amira al-Dahr and launched my consciousness across the
divide. However, since I hadn't been born yet in this new
timeline I had to wait. As the time got closer, I was able to
reach out to you in your dreams… and now here I am."

"I understand… completely," Hayden said. "I fully
comprehend every thought that went through your head,
every pain in your body, every feeling and emotion of

violation, confusion, betrayal, and helplessness. I know why you were so intent on killing Amaris on that terrace in Los Angeles. If I had known then what I know now, I would have let you. I would have helped you do it."

"You feel what I felt," Kinsley said. "You know what it is to be me. I feel bad for that, but at the same time I cherish the fact that you and I are so close. In the alternate timeline, I never let you know what was wrong with me. I never let you in, even though you could tell that something was wrong with me. I have always regretted that. You were always trying to be there for me… to be a safe haven for me. So even though it was painful and probably earth-shattering for you to experience it now, I needed to let you in. I needed you to understand. I want the relationship with you in this timeline that I didn't let the alternate versions of us have."

"That explains some things," Hayden said. "If you want, I can try to erase all of those memories from your mind."

"It's not necessary," Kinsley said. "When I crossed over to this timeline things changed. In the old timeline, I felt what you are feeling now. In this timeline though, I can remember it happening to alternate me… but I no longer feel like it actually happened *to me*. It's more like a nightmare that I can recall after waking up. It doesn't haunt me anymore. The trauma didn't follow me here."

"Thank God," Hayden said with a sigh of relief.

"Now that you know and understand, I can use the dreamscape to take the trauma from your mind also," Kinsley said. "You'll still remember it all, like a dream. You and I will still have the bond of e'it ad'a layadänte, so we will still share everything that goes along with that… but you won't have to feel that anguish anymore."

"I can…" Hayden started.

"You don't need to bear that weight on your shoulders," Kinsley interrupted him. "It's a noble enough gesture, but I no longer bear it and you don't need to either."

Before Hayden could respond, Kinsley reached out and touched his cheek. His eyelids fluttered closed and moments later he woke again.

"There, I did it," Kinsley said. "Nothing changed between us… it's just that the pain is gone."

"You are right," Hayden replied. "Thank you."

"Can you get me a glass of water?" Kinsley asked.

"Of course," Hayden said. "Come to think of it, I need something to drink also."

As Hayden filled two cups with water in the kitchen, Kinsley fidgeted around in the living room. Hayden came back and sat next to her on the couch.

"So, there is one more reason that I wanted you to

experience some of that," Kinsley admitted.

"Okay, what reason is that?" Hayden asked.

"The problems that you're having right now with Elle," she replied. "Before the part where Amaris attacked me, when I was just there in my bedroom. For a couple of minutes, you got to experience what it was like to be me… before all of the trauma. You were able to feel and fully comprehend what it is to be an eleven year old girl."

"Yeah, that was… different," Hayden said. "An entirely different world, honestly."

"All of those thoughts, feelings, and emotions that you experienced should give you some insight into what Elle is going through," Kinsley continued. "All of the things that she's feeling right now, stem from things she felt when she was that same age. She might hide them well, but she has self-confidence issues and fears of being left because of things that happened in her past."

"She did mention that," Hayden admitted.

"Okay, Dad," Kinsley said with a little sass in her voice. "Let's talk about Elle."

"Kinsley, I've ignored the past few times," Hayden replied. "But why do you insist on calling your mother by her first name?"

"Because she's not the mother that I knew," Kinsley

said. "The mother that I grew up with was strong and fierce. She didn't back down, she didn't hide out in a fancy house in Camarillo and leave her husband to take care of their youngest daughter by himself. This Elle is weak, indecisive, and petty. That's not my mother."

"Kinsley Rae!" Hayden said, a tinge of anger becoming apparent in his voice. "That is uncalled for."

"I'll give you a moment," Kinsley said and then sat silently.

Hayden took a deep breath and calmed himself before continuing. "Kins, when I saw you in those dreams and when I aged you up to help fight Amaris… you look exactly like your mother did when she was your age. I'm not saying that you look similar… you look like a clone of Elle when she was twelve. However, with how you act… that's where the similarities between you two seem to end. Understand me when I tell you that you would be extremely lucky to grow up to be like your mother. She is the most loyal, empathetic, and loving person that I have ever known. She is hard-working and smart. She has drive and passion. Your mother is perfect, Kinsley… and I don't say that in some sappy, half-true, trying to score points, greeting card kind of way. I say it with the utmost sincerity. It is a statement of absolute truth to me."

"Then why let Kali live?" Kinsley provoked. "If Elle is

so perfect to you, why the backup plan?"

"Do you want to know what I think about Kali?" Hayden asked. "About her compared to your mother? Is that what you're trying to get at? This is what I think… Kali who? Your mother is the only woman that occupies my mind. In a universe full of people, no one else comes within a light year of what Elle means to me."

"You think maybe that's why she brought up that night at the middle school dance when you two were arguing?" Kinsley prodded further.

"Were you listening to us the whole time?" Hayden asked, prompting an eye roll from Kinsley. "Oh, no, you just know… because you know. She did bring up that night. We talked about how her date left her on the dance floor for some other girl. We talked about after I picked her up and we spent the rest of the night together… and how special that made her feel."

"How special it made her feel," Kinsley repeated. "The things that you…"

"Did. For her," Hayden said, realizing that Kinsley had been baiting him and was leading the conversation the entire time to arrive at this point. "I showed her how special she was… how much she meant, through my actions."

"You can tell me that I'm your favorite daughter,"

Kinsley joked. "I promise that I won't tell Kiera."

"Yeah, I bet you'd stay totally silent," Hayden joked back. "I know what I can do, an action that I can take. One that doesn't involve killing anyone, but will still give Elle back a sense of control."

"Good," Kinsley replied. "Now let's talk about the future."

"It's all sunshine and rainbows, I presume," Hayden said sarcastically.

"That's the thing," Kinsley replied. "It is. At least as far as I can see. The troubling thing is, I can only see out for about six months. Then it all goes black. Every time I look, it's mostly the same… little pieces change because of the daily choices people make, but the overarching direction of time stays the same. I always come to an end on a seemingly normal day. I believe that it's a day in February because there are a bunch of red heart balloons, flowers, and stuff all throughout the day. You, me, Kiera, and Mom are at dinner having a great time. Then it just goes black… like time ends."

"That's…" Hayden began, but was at a loss for words. "What do you think it means? Time doesn't just end completely."

"The only logical conclusion that I can reach, is that I die," Kinsley said. "That I cannot see past that point because

I cease to exist."

"That doesn't make sense though," Hayden disagreed. "Bilv'at was able to see far into the future… far after when history tells us she died."

"Yes and no," Kinsley said. "The Amira al-Dahr can see into the future until the moment they die. There is an exception to the rule though. If they touch someone, they can see that person's future… even if it goes on after the Amira dies. Bilv'at ruled a great nation at one point. Every citizen was required to make a journey to the capital and bow to her. During that ceremony, she touched each person on the shoulder. She accumulated vast knowledge of the future just by doing that. Also, we know she was the original Amira al-Dahr… but we don't know *what* she actually was. Her other powers could have exceeded those that come with this title."

"Okay, well you can't see past that point normally," Hayden said as he took Kinsley's hand in his. "Here, you're touching me… look at my future. See if it goes past that point."

"Alright," Kinsley said. She closed her eyes and concentrated. A few moments later, she spoke again. "It ends at the same point in time."

"So allegedly something takes both *you* and *me* out at

the same time?" Hayden said doubtfully.

"I know, that doesn't seem likely at all," Kinsley agreed. "All I know is that whatever happens on that day is probably bad."

"We need to prepare ourselves," Hayden said. "If it's something that we can fight, then we have to fight."

"I agree," Kinsley said. "We can train together in the dreamscape. We can brainstorm ways to increase the strength of our powers."

"Okay," Hayden concurred. "Right now, let's get some sleep. Tomorrow morning we can go take care of things with Kali. After that, we will think more on this."

"Goodnight, Dad," Kinsley said as she stood and walked toward the spare bedroom. "I love you."

"Love you too, Kins," Hayden replied as he passed her on the way to his own bedroom.

෬ ෬ ෬ ෬ ෬ ෬

The Next Morning
Armond's Home

Kinsley sat in the passenger seat of the car, waiting for Hayden to get off the phone. The morning was cool and overcast.

Kinsley enjoyed the feeling of the almost damp air chilling her skin as she held her arm out the open window.

"Okay, thank you Mom," Hayden said into the phone. "I'll owe you one."

"Everything set?" Kinsley asked as Hayden hung up the phone.

"Yeah. Now to bring some resolution to this situation," Hayden said as they stepped out of the car and walked to Armond's front door.

"Come on in," Armond said as he opened the door. "Kali and Paige are on the back patio."

"Good morning," Hayden said to everyone as he stepped out onto the patio with Kinsley and Armond.

"Paige has been telling me about your idea," Kali said to Hayden. "She seems to think that it's a good idea."

"What do you think?" Hayden asked her.

"I think that I want to talk to you alone," Kali replied.

"Okay, no problem," Hayden said as he waved everyone back inside the house and sat down next to Kali.

"So tell me what the plan is," Kali said. "Paige told me, but I want to make sure she got everything right."

"My parents own several houses in the Las Vegas area," Hayden began. "They also own several different businesses. Some IT offices, a couple restaurants, and a sign company.

They have a vacant house that you can stay in, with no rent for the first three months. There's also a management position waiting for you at one of their companies. My father knows a lot of people over at UNLV, so if you want to continue school, he can get you in no problem. Paige and Armond will come check in with you at least once a month… and my parents are only about five miles away from where you'd be. I don't know if you remember Clark and Samantha, but his job is relocating him from Chicago to Las Vegas. They are good friends, Paige knows them well."

"I mean, it sounds like a great opportunity," Kali said. "Honestly, I don't even know why I'm in Fullerton… other than to visit Paige. You and your family have always been great. You've always been a wonderful friend, ever since we were little kids. I'm wondering though, is all of this happening because of what I said to Abby? I know that I overstepped and it was a stupid thing to say, especially with your wife in the house. I just suddenly had these feelings for you. They kind of came out of nowhere."

"Kali, I have loved having you and Paige in my life," Hayden replied. "Like you said, we've all been close friends since we were little. If you have feelings for me… I know that's something that you can't control, but it would probably be best for both of us if we weren't constantly around each other. I have to focus on my family. I love Elle and no person or thing is ever going to come before her. I don't mean to come off harsh, but there is no chance for anything between you and I. As a friend, I just want you to hear that first-hand from me so there is no confusion."

"Are we still going to be friends?" Kali asked.

"You'll always be a friend to me," Hayden said. "Will we see each other or talk on the phone? I wouldn't count on it. Elle is allowed to dictate those boundaries and I will respect them. I am sure that Paige and Armond will let you know how everyone is doing when they visit… and I'm sure they will relay how you are doing to me, Dan, and Abby."

"Thank you for being honest and clear with me," Kali said. "It's actually refreshing in a world full of people that seem to just lead you on and then ghost you. You're a great person and Elle is an extremely lucky girl. I will take the offer from your parents. I'll have Paige drive me and the baby out to Vegas this afternoon. I guess this is goodbye then?"

"I suppose so," Hayden agreed. "Go out there and do great things. I know you will. Goodbye, Kali."

"Goodbye," she echoed with a heavy sigh.

Hayden stepped back inside and signaled Paige to go back out to the patio with her sister. Kinsley and Armond followed Hayden outside to the driveway.

"She's going?" Armond asked.

"She is," Hayden replied. "Paige is going to take her this afternoon."

"Well, I am glad that all worked out," Armond said. "It is for the best. I will keep you updated on my observations."

"Thank you, Armond," Hayden said as he opened the car door. "I will see you later."

The car ride between Armond's home and the apartment was unusually quiet. Kinsley held her arm out the window, still enjoying the damp morning air. As they arrived at the apartment she finally spoke.

"You're an amazing father," Kinsley said to Hayden. "You are an outstanding husband. You are a great man."

"Thank you," Hayden replied almost inquisitively, a little taken aback by Kinsley's sudden barrage of compliments.

"I just want you to know that," Kinsley continued. "It doesn't matter which reality or timeline we're in… you have always been amazing. You've always been there for me. I can tell that you care about me deeply… and about Mom and Kiera too. You're my role model, my example of how a man should treat a woman, my safety, and my refuge. You are the standard to which I hold people. Not surprisingly, most people don't measure up. Actually, no one does."

Hayden let go of the car door handle and took in

the words that Kinsley had said. As his words failed him, he simply cried for a few moments.

"Kins," he finally said. "I'd say that you don't know how much that means to me… but you probably do know. Thank you. I love you."

"Go ahead and go inside," Kinsley said. "I'll be in soon."

Hayden nodded, collected himself, and exited the car. As soon as he was inside, Kinsley got out of the car and opened a portal to Camarillo.

℘ ℘ ℘ ℘ ℘ ℘

"Knock, knock," Kinsley said in a raised voice as she tapped her fist against the front door of their home in Camarillo.

"Kinsley?" Elle said confused as she looked around the front yard to see if she was alone. "What are you doing here?"

"I need to talk to you, Mom," Kinsley replied. "I have something that you need to hear also."

"Okay," Elle said, still quite confused. "Come on in."

Kinsley sat on the couch next to Elle and pulled out the tablet that her and Kiera had been playing with the previous day. She loaded the voice recorder app and set the tablet on the coffee table.

"What is this?" Elle asked before Kinsley played the audio.

"I recorded mine and Dad's conversation last night," Kinsley admitted.

"What?" Elle asked. "Does he know you recorded him?"

"Nope," she admitted. "I'm sure he'll forgive me though. Just listen."

"Fine," Elle acquiesced.

"Just so you know, Mom," Kinsley added. "All of the things that I say about you in this recording… I don't mean them. I was just trying to make Dad speak his unfiltered truth, which he did. I know that I've kind of acted like a jerk to you and I'm sorry. I love you, Mom."

Before Elle could respond, Kinsley hit the play button on the tablet's screen. Elle listened to the conversation, occasionally looking up at Kinsley with a frown at some of her remarks. At the end of the recording, Elle's face seemed to have softened and she let out a long sigh.

"Armond and Paige are taking Kali out to Las Vegas this afternoon," Kinsley said. "She's moving there permanently. Your husband took action… he is showing you that you're more important to him than anything else."

"Thank you, Kinsley," Elle said. "You really care about

your father."

"I really care about you too, Mom," Kinsley corrected. "I know that sometimes I'm a little unorthodox with my methods, but that's because I see the path to the destination when other people cannot. Sometimes that makes people uncomfortable or makes them think that I'm aloof and don't care for them."

"Why don't you head back to Fullerton," Elle suggested. "Spend the rest of the day with your father and then come back here in the evening. Both of you. Kiera and I are going to make dinner. We can all have a nice meal together… as a family."

"We will be here," Kinsley agreed. "I was going to make him take me to the beach today anyway, so we can clear our minds of the past few days."

"Oh, while you're here, I still have the box of my old clothes out," Elle said. "You've been wearing the same thing since before the fight in Los Angeles."

"Oh yeah, I guess that I have," Kinsley replied as she looked down at her dirty and tattered clothes.

"Here we go," Elle said as she rummaged through the box. "A clean shirt and some pants… here's a hoodie too since it's unusually cold this morning. Oh, and here's one of my old bikinis if you want it. That water is always freezing cold to me, but just in case."

"Thanks, Mom," Kinsley said as she took the stack of clothes. "I'll be back with Dad this evening. Love you."

"Love you too," Elle replied as Kinsley opened a portal and then disappeared from the living room.

ᴆ ᴆ ᴆ ᴆ ᴆ ᴆ

"Mom wants us to come to the house for dinner tonight," Kinsley told Hayden as she lay on a beach towel in the swimsuit Elle had given her.

"You talked to your mother?" Hayden asked.

"Yeah, what did you think I was doing earlier after you went inside?" Kinsley joked. "Where did you think I got this bikini from?"

"I don't know, I thought maybe you were doing normal things… not meddling," Hayden joked back. "And I figured you had gone through some of the backup clothes left at the apartment. Speaking of the bikini, aren't you cold out here? It looks like it's going to rain."

"I'm a little cold," Kinsley replied as she stood up. "But I've never been to the beach before. So I'm going to ignore that."

"You want me to go with you?" Hayden asked as

Kinsley started taking steps toward the ocean.

"Yeah, of course," she said and then took off running toward the waves.

Hayden stood and ran after her into the water. The chill immediately reminded him why he preferred to swim in the oceans surrounding more tropical destinations. After a moment to adjust, Hayden bucked up and leapt into an approaching wave.

"Wow, that is freezing!" Hayden said as he reappeared above the water's surface.

"And yet you're still out here with me," Kinsley said. "Thank you."

"I wouldn't miss your first time in the ocean, even if this was ice water," Hayden told her.

ങ ങ ങ ങ ങ ങ

Hayden and Kinsley arrived back at the Fullerton apartment in the mid-afternoon. After a quick snack, each of them took a shower to wash off the salt and sand. Kinsley sat still in thought on the carpet in front of Hayden as he brushed out her hair.

"Any ideas on the future?" she asked as Hayden began putting her hair into a braid.

"Maybe," Hayden replied. "Your vision of the future assumes that we both die… probably in some sudden catastrophic event. We don't have to die though. We can circumvent that reality easily."

"You want to cast that spell Bilv'at taught you?" Kinsley asked, knowing exactly what Hayden was alluding to. "Are you prepared to live that long? What about Mom and Kiera?"

"I don't know," Hayden admitted. "But if we're going to survive to defeat whatever threat is coming, then we have to live through whatever moment is coming for us. We could always reverse the spell afterwards."

"Dad, there's only one way to reverse the effects of that spell," Kinsley said. "If you cast the rending spell, then we will lose all of our powers. All of them."

"Would that be such a bad thing?" Hayden asked. "After we are all safe… to just live a normal life."

"Are we ever going to really be safe?" Kinsley argued. "If you don't have your powers, you can't protect Mom or us as well as you can now. Some random maniac with a gun or knife could kill you."

"We can cross that bridge when we come to it," Hayden said, still undecided on what he wanted. "My second idea was about the strength of our powers. We need to be at our peak to fight this unknown threat. My amulet amplifies our powers… but now we have Amaris' amulet also. What if we combined them into one?"

"We can both draw off the combined amulet's power," Kinsley said, considering the idea. "When Amaris went back in time and drew off energy from the Alva'ci, he didn't get quite as much power as your amulet holds… but it will still be a significant upgrade. Any increase in power reserves will be very helpful with an unknown threat."

"Let's do it then," Hayden said as he placed a hair tie at the end of Kinsley's completed braid and then pulled the amulet out from underneath his shirt. "The other amulet is on the nightstand in my bedroom."

After Kinsley took a moment to admire her hair in a hand mirror, they ventured into the bedroom and Hayden handed Amaris' amulet to her. They placed both stones together and cupped their hands together around them. As they focused on their powers, the stones began to glow brilliantly. Flashes of orange and purple pulsed throughout the room until they gave way to pure white light. As the intensity grew, the ground beneath the apartment began shaking. A minute later, a sharp tremor that was felt for dozens of miles jolted through the earth. The white light encompassing the melding amulets pulsed like a miniature star. The heat that radiated from the stones soon became unbearable to hold. Hayden and Kinsley removed their hands, letting the stones float in place as they joined together.

"It's starting to hurt… a lot!" Kinsley screamed.

The power rolled off the amulet in waves, each stronger than the last… and each one hitting father and daughter like a forceful punch square in the chest. Hayden became worried about their ability to withstand the growing impacts. Kinsley's nose began bleeding after several more waves of growing power hit her. Soon after, Hayden coughed a handful of blood into his palm.

"It's too much, Dad!" Kinsley yelled, her voice now wavering.

"I can't stop it!" Hayden yelled back as he unsuccessfully attempted to halt the fusion of the amulets.

"Do something, please!" Kinsley pleaded as blood started to steadily drip from her ears as well. "I can't hold on for much longer."

Hayden took several labored steps toward Kinsley. The amulet's field of power had made it difficult to move. Her body was beginning to sway back and forth, signaling an impending loss of consciousness. Hayden wrapped his arms tightly around Kinsley. He was not sure if his last-minute idea would have any effect as he felt his own consciousness slipping away from him. He kissed Kinsley on the forehead as he held her. If he was about to die, this was a final action that he could die at peace with.

"Chronish'navaya," Hayden whispered before everything went black.

Epilogue

Say My Name

54,000 BC

Bilv'at took a seat on the terrace of her estate and looked out over the gulf. The once small settlement she established had grown from a sparse collection of tents into a sprawling urban center. Her meager dwelling had long since been torn down. In its stead, an enormous palace stood. The white stone that comprised the palatial estate was complimented with brightly colored tiles on the pillars and balconies.

"Come and sit next to me," Bilv'at told her follower Shamiyah. "Enjoy the view with me on my last day here."

"Yes, Sultana," Shamiyah replied. "Let me just gather your meal and I will be right there."

"Make sure that you prepare yourself something to eat as well," Bilv'at said. "...and pour yourself a glass of wine."

Shamiyah brought several plates to the small table next to Bilv'at and sat down in a chair as instructed. She began nibbling on her meal as Bilv'at continued to look out at the water in silence.

"Today, you shall forgo the rest of your duties and keep me company," Bilv'at said. "You have been a loyal and close friend throughout the years."

"Thank you," Shamiyah replied. "I truly wish that you did not have to depart. The kingdom will surely miss your guidance and leadership."

"I leave the kingdom in capable hands," Bilv'at said. As if on cue, Saleem Amman rounded the corner and approached. "In fact, there he is now. Come and join us, Saleem."

"Sultana Bilv'at," Saleem replied. "It would be my honor. The city is prepared for your departure. We will all mourn your absence."

"You will be perfectly fine without me," Bilv'at told him. "You have learned from me over the past two thousand years. I trust that you have acquired the wisdom and discernment to lead this great kingdom."

———

"I will continue to teach my eldest to rule in my place when that day comes," Saleem said.

"That is imperative," Bilv'at concurred. "I can sense the imminent arrival of the Alva'ci on this planet. Once the fight between the creature and the people of el-Abbasil concludes, the power that has extended all of your lifetimes will come to an end. You should have another thirty to fifty years of life left within you. However, after living this long, that time will pass like a blink of an eye."

"We will not fail you, Sultana," Saleem said. "May your new kingdom flourish and prosper as this one has."

"I apologize for being late," a man said to the group on the terrace as he hurriedly approached. His striking good looks drew the attention of everyone present, a fact of life that he had grown accustomed to over the years. "Please forgive me. I was delayed in a conversation with one of my daughter's teachers."

"Worry not," Bilv'at replied. "All is forgiven Fariq 'awal Constralis. Your instrumental role in the success of this empire will be remembered for all time. Come and join us. I was just about to explain my plans for the future."

"Antonus Constralis, the father of nations, how are you on this fine evening?" Saleem asked as the newcomer settled into a nearby chair.

"All is well," Antonus replied. "The city is flourishing, my wives and children are all in good health, and reports from the battlefield are overwhelmingly positive. I have nothing to complain about."

"Sultana Bilv'at, would you care for more wine?" Shamiyah asked, noticing that her cup was empty.

"Shamiyah, pass the pitcher to me. I will pour my own wine," Bilv'at replied. "Remember, I excused you from your duties for the remainder of the day."

"Apologies, Sultana," Shamiyah said. "A force of habit, I'm afraid."

"No need to apologize," Bilv'at told her. "Since we are disregarding formalities, both of you can drop the titles and the decorum that goes along with it. Call me by my real name."

"As you wish, Asbeel," Saleem replied. "May you reign for ten thousand more years."

"We can certainly hope for that reality," she responded. "At the conclusion of the night, I will use my powers to project my being forward in time. Unfortunately, this will result in the dissolution of my physical body. However, I have identified a suitable host in the future to inhabit. With this new body, I will raise a new army, reestablish our empire, and expand the borders across the entire planet."

"An ambitious plan in a new time period," Saleem said. "I have no doubt about your ability to achieve it."

"Thank you, my friend and advisor," Bilv'at replied. "I am sorry that you will not be alive to share in the splendor of the new empire."

"I am certain that you will amass new allies to your cause," Saleem said.

"What will you do until the day comes?" Bilv'at asked, now speaking to Antonus.

"I will remain here in Elath, at least until all of my children are grown. I will assist Saleem with the defense and operations of the city and empire." Antonus replied. "After that, I will most likely wander until I find a worthy distraction. Perhaps even rejoin our brethren for a while if they need my aid. Once you reappear, I will come to your side if you beckon me to."

"I would certainly welcome your assistance," she replied. "We rebelled together. Let us rise together again in the future."

"Will you seek out the others?" Antonus asked.

"My relationship with the others is much more strained than yours," Bilv'at answered. "We can probably manage on our own, though I have entertained the thought of enlisting the help of Mammon."

"We should avoid that at all costs," Antonus advised. "He is unpredictable and acts only in his own interests."

"I know as well as you do," Bilv'at replied. "I will make my determination once I have met and assessed our foes."

ↄ ↄ ↄ ↄ ↄ ↄ

Armond pressed play on his television remote and enjoyed the plush comfort of his couch. He savored the moment of relaxation, a rare luxury in his new reality. In the dimmed light of the living room, the screen flashed to life and the roar of audio that accompanied the opening credits to a movie filled the room.

"I could get used to this," Armond said to himself. "Peace, quiet, actual personal time."

Ten minutes into the film, Armond reached for the glass of water on the coffee table. As his hand drew near to it, he squinted to look at the cup. The surface of the water appeared to be dancing about ever-so-slightly. As he took a drink of water, Armond paused the movie and turned the lights in the living room back on.

"Already?" he asked aloud, wondering if the moment of respite was going to be more brief than he had envisioned.

A small tremor rolled through the ground beneath his home and seemed to answer his question. Armond looked around the room, hoping that this was just an ordinary earthquake. He wanted nothing more than to finally sit down and watch his current movie selection. He stood in silence for a few moments before a jarring jolt of energy shook the ground violently.

"I knew it was too good to be true," Armond again spoke aloud to himself.

As he looked out the front window of his home, a bright flash of white light raced across the sky. It could easily have been mistaken for lightning, except that there were no clouds in the sky... and Armond had a gnawing hunch that this was something more sinister. He attempted to reach out to Hayden telepathically.

"Nothing," he said after a few moments of trying. "I better go over there and check on him."

Armond grasped his car keys in his hand and turned to make his way toward the front door when he heard a familiar sound... a sound that shouldn't be occurring. He looked back at the door to his safe and confirmed that it was ajar. An uneasy feeling grew in his stomach as he slowly walked over to the safe and pulled the door open.

On the upper shelf near the back sat a book, separated from all the others. It was nondescript and unimportant. Armond had placed it alone due to the fact that both its cover and pages were completely blank. His father had insisted that the book belong with the others, so Armond did as he was instructed and kept it in his safe.

"What is this?" Armond asked himself, his voice now higher-pitched than normal.

The cover of the blank book started to glow as a title began to appear on its surface, as if it were being etched into the leather by an invisible fiery pen. Armond grabbed the book from the back of the safe and pulled it out. As he flipped through the pages, he found chapters of text had also appeared out of thin air. Armond clasped the book shut and read the cover aloud, "al-Malhama al-Dunyā."

"That is not good," Armond said after a brief pause to collect his thoughts.

He tucked the book under his arm, closed the safe, and then rushed out the door. As someone known for his patience and moderation, the fact that Armond was driving toward Hayden's apartment at twenty-five miles per hour over the speed limit indicated the urgency and fear that he now felt.

Armond pulled into the driveway behind Hayden's car and rushed to exit the vehicle. An uneasy feeling washed over him as he walked up to the front door of the apartment.

"Hello?" he called out as he opened the door.

No answer. It was evident that someone was there or had been recently. The lights throughout the home were on and Kinsley's damp towel was still draped over the back of a chair in the living room. Armond slowly walked down the hallway toward Hayden's bedroom, listening for any sounds that might give him a clue.

As Armond cracked open the bedroom door and peered inside, the first object that jumped into his vision was the amulet. It floated in the middle of the room, shining with a bright white light. Armond reached for his phone and put it on speakerphone.

"Elle," he stuttered after she picked up. "Can you come down to Fullerton right now? Something has happened to Hayden and Kinsley."

Appendix I

The Ancient Powers

The several powers, or magical abilities, are first seen in use in 54,000 BC (see Agents of Fate: Chapter Three). At that point in time, they became dormant in humans due to a spell performed by Abbas. Their traces were passed on, although they were undetectable to their bearers and the powers unusable.

In 2022, a prophecy came true when Hayden de Vere turned out to be the foretold cognizant one. The appearance of the cognizant one was prophesied by Abbas in a vision approximately two years after the Alva'ci came to Earth. As the bearers of the dormant powers began to die off in 2022, the powers began to manifest once again in their real forms.

Little information is known about the origination of the magical abilities and how or when humans acquired them. It is rumored that there is a book of lore, written by Abbas when he was close to his death, that conveys the secrets that humans used to acquire their magical abilities. Whether or not this book exists is known only to the descendants of Abbas.

The Powers and Their Symbols:

Elemental Powers:

Water ماء   Fire نار

Earth أرض   Air جو

Sub-Elemental Powers:

Light ضوء   Energy طاقة

Shadow ظل   Electricity برق

Non-Elemental Powers:

Ane'illuminus / Thought خاطِر

The Seven Spells نوبات

The Seven Spells:

Abarus - Otherworldly Warriors

Tithethus - The Bindings

Emiratus - Power Amplification

Prophesch'naya Con'di Ashante - Shroud of Darkness
Chantiatus - Protective Forcefields
Youlvasius - Lucky Strikes
Amal Esta Preavius - Energy Portals

The Eighth Spell:
Nelitus Absoritum Malitus - Alva'ci Banishment

The Forbidden Spell:
E'it ad'a Layadänte

Appendix II

The Prophecies

Abbas recorded several prophecies and visions shortly before he passed away. The following selections are relevant to this entry in The Agents of Fate Series.

The Abassilon Prophecy
53993 BC

At once, you awake and find yourself in a new world,
a new beginning.
The scars of time, though stinging at times,
are dulled from passing years.
Memories of nights that shall never be forgotten
flash through your mind from time to time,
to remind you of all that was had, of all that was lost.

You walk upon the sands,
on the beach of this new land..
journeying to something yet unknown.
You see a girl, standing alone by the water's edge.
Her golden hair flowing in the breeze, her voice fair and sweet.
Her eyes, while calm and inviting,
also piercing and hiding much behind them.

As you walk nearer, flashes of destiny
race through your mind like precognitive deja vu.
What path is coming to emerge?
You can feel it in your bones,
if you approach her, a piece of your life will be hers.

They've called you many things...
they focused on the darkness that swirled around you.
And though they were mistaken,
as magnificence can oft be mistook for darkness,
they never understood.
But as you look onward toward the girl,
you can see the light from within her.

...and the light shall mingle with the darkness, and together
they shall shine with a brilliance both dazzling and fearsome.

———

She turns to see you and you look into her eyes.
Suddenly you understand,
and together you walk toward the city.

~~E'it ad'a layadänte~~
We shall share this path

The Prophecy of Hindrant Salvas
53980 BC

Pacing the grounds, hollow footsteps echo into oblivion.
Turning round, facing the reality of duplicity.

Into the waters, knee-deep. The rip current drawing you in.
The seduction that you both play on each other
is providential.

What can you have?
Is it greater than anything you've been given?
What remains to be seen,
shall determine the course of revisionist history.

Turning a corner into the halls of life yet written.
Through the doorway and into an empty room.

We have come to dance here,
a dance careful and indifferent.
Setting the night ablaze with aberrant passions.
The world outside these windows, vast and insignificant.
Who you are at dusk is not the you of dawn.

Reaching a precipice, fraught with lasting decisions.
How do you get what you want,
when what you want is everything?

Appendix III

The Books of Lore

Abbas wrote several books that were passed down to the firstborn of each generation of his family. These books contained the lore concerning the Agents of Fate. The current keeper of the books of lore is Armond el-Hashem. Among the known volumes are:

The Conqueror الفاتح

An account of the arrival of the Alva'ci on Earth. This book contains first-hand accounts from Abbas, Ahjiamed, Koshili, and dozens of other members of their village. Also included are charts and drawings depicting the creature, a sky chart detailing where the Alva'ci entered the atmosphere, and a description of the orange rock that the creature's armor consisted of.

Prophecies and Visions نبوءات ورؤى

After the victory obtained over the Alva'ci in 54,000 BC, Abbas began to have visions pertaining to the nature of the Agents of Fate and future events that concerned those that held the remnants of power. This book of lore is a collection of the visions and prophecies that Abbas made until his death at the age of 387. One of the most prominent prophecies included was The Parisifian Prophecy. This prophecy foretold the eventual appearance of the Cognizant One, an Agent of Fate that was unique in their abilities and would come at a time in history when the Alva'ci may possess the ability to rise again.

Powers and Practices القدرات والمهارات
(aka Abilities and Skills)

Written very late in the life of Abbas, this book of lore's existence is only rumored. It is said that this book includes detailed explanations of how humans first acquired magical abilities. Details of each magical power and its uses are included, ranging from the simplest forms to advanced techniques that came with aptitude and skill. The book includes a detailed account of the power of Ane'illuminus and the achievements made by those that mastered the power within their lifetimes. A section of the lore includes an account of how Abbas and a handful of others were able to artificially extend their lives to seemingly unnatural ages through the masterful use of the magical powers. Finally, Abbas included warnings concerning the use of The Forbidden Spell (which is mentioned in The Abassilon Prophecy, but with the words crossed out to prevent its use). The warnings also included several accounts of various magic users that attempted the spell only to meet their immediate deaths.

Appendix IV

Glossary

'Ain Ghazal – an ancient city, located near modern-day Amman in Jordan.

A'ltal Bilv'at – a power of unknown origin or use, mentioned by Ahjiamed in 54,000 BC.

Alva'ci – A species of alien lifeform. Origin unknown. The term is also used to identify the singular creature that arrived on planet Earth in 54,000 BC (The Alva'ci).

Amulet, The – A transformation of the shard that enhances its power through a more perfect shape.

Ane'illuminus – One of the non-elemental powers. This power deals with the Mind/Thought. The wielder of this power can utilize the dreamscape and has precognitive dreams.

Elath – an ancient city that encompassed what would be modern-day Aqaba, Jordan and Eilat, Israel.

Fariq – a military rank, second only to the Fariq ' awal.

Fariq 'awal – the highest military rank in the Empire of 'Ain Ghazal.

Appendix V

Antonus

Antonus Constralis, the father of nations, the esteemed Fariq 'awal of 'Ain Ghazal and the Dominion of Bilv'at, an abridged genealogy:

Among the eight tribes of Elath, Antonus took thirty wives. With the families of Elath's aristocracy and upper-class, Antonus took another twenty wives.

From the tribe of Surethi, Antonus wed the daughters Zurina, Khadija, Alya, and Raisa. From Antonus and his wives of Surethi lineage, twenty-four children were born.

From the tribe of Ayada, Antonus wed the daughters Asra and Manoush. From Antonus and his wives of Ayada lineage, thirteen children were born.

From the tribe of Coppolas, Antonus wed the daughters

Widjan, Jinan, Soraya, and Mumina. From Antonus and his wives of Coppolas lineage, twenty-five children were born.

From the tribe of Hurym, Antonus wed the daughters Mina, Almas, and Zafina. From Antonus and his wives of Hurym lineage, twenty-seven children were born.

From the tribe of Norwan, Antonus wed the daughters Jamila, Sumayya, Zulekha, Aaliyah, and Zani. From Antonus and his wives of Norwan lineage, forty children were born.

From the tribe of Retamini, Antonus wed the daughters Fatin, Sara, Ismat, and Jacinta. From Antonus and his wives of Retamini lineage, thirty-seven children were born.

From the tribe of Rylissilin, Antonus wed the daughters Isa, Sanaa, Aliyya, and Zulema. From Antonus and his wives of Rylissilin lineage, thirty-five children were born.

From the tribe of Tannisha, Antonus wed the daughters Aisha, Khalilah, Fizza, and Jalila. From Antonus and his wives of Tannisha lineage, thirty-three children were born.

Altogether, the wives from the tribes of Elath bore Antonus

two hundred and thirty-three children.

From other families in Elath, Antonus wed:

Isra Anvyen and Xaviera Anvyen
Eshe Avadi, Safa Avadi, and Yusra Avadi
Hooda Damari, Ihsan Damari, and Sumayah Damari
Karida Frism and Samia Frism
Alyssia Lendela, Hadya Lendela, and Haniyya Lendela
Farah Malandor, Yasmeen Malandor, and Rihanna Malandor
Dalal Norvandrel and Azalea Norvandrel
Rifat Slanthar and Asha Slanthar

These wives bore Antonus one hundred and thirty children.

The children of Antonus in the City of Elath produced a total of 1125 grandchildren. The sixth generation from Antonus totaled 171,406 descendants.

Though this document only covers the activities of Antonus in the City of Elath, it is worth mentioning that he also took wives in the cities of ʿAin Ghazal, Madinah, and Riyadh. Those wives bore him similar numbers of children in each city.

About the Author

Tony Contratto writes books, this much we know. He is also the owner of *Styles AZ* in Lake Havasu City and a nonprofit director.

Tony's philosophy is that the most gripping and immersive tales happen in our imagination. Tony spent several years formulating the story of his first novel within his head, before ever putting the proverbial pen to paper. After the conclusion of the fifth book in the Agents of Fate Series, Tony will focus on an adjacent story entitled *Squandered Light*. Originally from Southern California, Tony now resides in Arizona. Visit Tony at his website and follow him on social media at contrattos.net

Coming Soon

Not all those who come bearing gifts are friends

With a devastating battle only days behind them… Hayden de Vere, his family, and friends are still coping with the remnants of physical and emotional trauma. Glimmers of hope and light provide only fleeting peace as the world sees the return of a threat whose existence had long ago been relegated to myths and legends. Hayden and Kinsley will face their greatest test yet, when they find that power alone may not be

enough to prevail.

Join Hayden, Elle, Abby, and Dan as
The Agents of Fate Series
continues with the **fifth** installment:

Child of Hope

"I changed things. To me, it was the only choice that I had."

❦ ❦ ❦ ❦ ❦ ❦

Sign up for the Insider Email Newsletter and receive
a FREE exclusive copy of the prequel story
AOF: The Distant Shadow

at

agentsoffate.com

More To Read

The Agents of Fate Series

begins with

Agents of Fate

*"Really enjoyed! Right from the beginning the story drew me in.
After that, every chapter ended with me not wanting to put it down."*

☙ ☙ ☙ ☙ ☙ ☙

Set fifteen years before Book One,
make sure to read the prequel story

The Distant Shadow

☙ ☙ ☙ ☙ ☙ ☙

Thank you for reading!

If you enjoyed this book, please take a moment to
add a review on Amazon and/or Goodreads.